Jack Simile and the Phantom Fury

Kelly Cheek

Cover and book design by Kelly Cheek

ISBN: 978-0-9909982-6-6

Fiery Muse Publishing
Littleton, Colorado 80129

Printed in the United States of America

Also by Kelly Cheek

All We Hold Dear

Trial by Fire

The Lost Colony

Profile

Private Messages

Poked

"Reality is merely an illusion, albeit a very persistent one."

Albert Einstein

The electronic tones on my phone jerked me awake. I reached over and turned the alarm off, then rolled back. At four o'clock on a morning in January, the only light in the room came from my phone. I slid my hand slowly to the side a little, and I sighed when I felt nothing but cold sheets.

I figured it must have been the argument last night that did it. Things had been tough with Becky lately. I thought that when we went to bed, we had gotten things worked out. But apparently, Becky had not been as satisfied with the outcome. She had left sometime in the night.

I pulled myself up and out of bed. With a quick, absent-minded movement, I flipped the covers up over the pillow and the bed was "made." As made as I ever did anyway. As I walked past the thermostat, I punched the button a couple of times to get the heat to come on, then went into the kitchen to start the coffee brewing.

My morning ablutions took only a few minutes. When I returned to the kitchen fully dressed, I poured a cup of coffee, and as I began my routine of assembling my lunch, I thought about the night before.

My name is Jack Hobbes. Despite having spent a good portion of my adolescence on a steady diet of super hero comic books, thrillers and science fiction novels, the fact was that my real life was pretty mundane. There were several details about my life that I would definitely change if I could, and routines, I told myself, helped me cope with what I *couldn't* change. Routines were comfortable.

Becky, though, seemed to be getting frustrated with me. I had worked for the same company for over ten years. While she originally thought that indicated a certain amount of stability, the fact that, at thirty-five years old, I was still working the same *job*, in the shipping department of a national snack food manufacturer, now looked to her, rather, as proof of a lack of ambition. I had to admit that there may be something to that.

At the same time, I just really disliked change.

I lived on what used to be a sugar beet farm in Weld County, north of Denver, Colorado. I had inherited the property after the death of my parents. As the sole survivor of the Hobbes lineage, I had been living in my childhood home for several years now. I had voluntarily left the farming way of life, though, one change that I *had* been happy to make, so I had gradually sold off all the land except for the house itself.

My parents had been very religious, and had brought me up according to their strict Christian lifestyle, complete with family prayer and a daily discussion of Bible texts. One complaint I frequently heard from my father was, "I wish you could remember scriptures like you remember lines from your novels." I had a quotation for practically any occasion. And a pretty decent vocabulary for a country kid.

Our Christian lifestyle also included a complete immersion of ourselves in our work. My parents felt that, as the Bible said, "if any would not work, neither should he eat." We liked to eat, so we worked our farm.

My heart had never been in it, though. The religion or the farming. Since my folks have been gone, I've been divesting myself of both, and feeling an endless supply of guilt about it. Those daily customs, though, were likely what started my own routines. My memory wasn't that great, but if you're in a routine, you don't have to remember as much.

I poured another cup of coffee and turned the coffee maker off. Then, I spilled some Froot Loops into a bowl and splashed some milk over it. Becky had once accused me of choosing what cereal I have for breakfast based on what day it was. I don't think I was really *that* tied to routine.

I pondered the Bible verse that had come to mind, about eating and working. That still happened fairly frequently. A text would pop into my head pertinent to whatever I was going through or thinking about. If my dad could see me now! Often, accompanying the verse would be a resurgence of guilt that I wasn't religious anymore. It had been a part of my life for so long, I couldn't seem to shake the guilt. I hoped that, if God was really up there, he was as forgiving as I had been taught.

Other changes were not so easy to live with. Due to some unfortunate financial decisions, and the recent end of an even more unfortunate marriage, money was tight. My credit had recently taken a tumble thanks to a couple of missed payments on my home. My routines seemed like a form of reassuring self-preservation.

When Becky entered my life, she first thought my routines were funny, quirky. Lately, though, she was beginning to think that "routines" wasn't accurate. She had dropped a few letters from the word and just called them ruts.

I placed my bowl in the sink and ran a little water into it while I finished my coffee. I dragged my feet into the bathroom and brushed my teeth, turned the thermostat back down and pulled on a coat. I picked up my insulated lunch bag and my keys and went outside, pulling the locked door shut behind me. It tended to stick a little, something I had been meaning to fix for the last few months, so I had to pull hard.

I barely noticed the scenery passing by as I drove to work. There wasn't much scenery to be seen anyway, as it was five o'clock in the morning, and still dark. But even if it had been light out, the county road I had driven every day for the past decade was so familiar that it likely wouldn't even have registered on my consciousness.

My car was a 1978 Plymouth Fury. That was the last year they made them, and it might have been considered a classic if it was in halfway decent shape. As it was, the car was a mottled patchwork of colors. The car used to be gold, but the front right and rear left fender panels, as well as the hood, had been transplanted from other cars in salvage yards over the course of a few years. Even so, the entire car was fairly consistently covered in rust, with some patches of it having eaten all the way through the metal.

I continued making my way south and west on the deserted county roads until I merged onto I-25 south. Even here, among the heavier traffic, though, my mind was still on Becky and our fight the night before.

Within a few minutes, I pulled off onto my exit from "elevated I-70," a stretch of the interstate east of downtown Denver that makes its way above a largely industrial chunk of the city. With the traffic continuing on its way above me, I pulled into the parking lot at a large building, completely generic-looking except for the big colorful SnakZone sign. I parked my car and gathered up my stuff.

This was my morning, pretty much every day. I didn't even have to think about it.

See what I mean? Pretty boring.

The day passed much like any other day. Pallets in the shipping department were stacked with boxes of chips and crackers and cookies, arranged according to the various customer orders, and I packed them into cartons for shipping. True to my nature, I had gradually developed a number of routines for things I did on a regular basis, and because of those, I was able to accomplish my work quickly. It was mundane work, but it didn't require much thinking on my part, and before I knew it, it was eleven o'clock.

Working such an early shift, lunch time came early for me. I didn't mind. I usually had the lunch room to myself. But lunch time gave me more time to think, and as I ate the lunch I had packed a few hours before, I found myself thinking again about Becky.

We had met several months before when mutual friends decided that we would be perfect for each other. Fairly fresh from my recent divorce, I wasn't so sure I was ready to meet someone new, but on the double date that our friends set up, I met and liked Becky Barlow instantly. I told her I thought she had the alliterative appellation of a comic book character.

Becky was a little country girl with a pretty face and a light smattering of freckles across her nose. Her thick, dark hair was usually pulled back into a braid. Despite having been raised in the country, she had a particularly urban way about her, which she said she got from her mother. She was an intelligent and eloquent woman, and she moved with a graceful sensuality that I found particularly intriguing.

Her mother had died when she was young, so she had been raised primarily by her father. He had worked in various places around Denver and Boulder, but their home had always been in the country, so they could see the stars.

Entering this new relationship with me, she was cautious, having endured a pair of bad marriages herself, so our relationship had begun slowly. We went out to dinner a couple of times before she invited me to dinner at her place. Feeling compelled to reciprocate, I invited Becky over for hamburgers.

It was a few weeks before we felt comfortable spending the night together, and even then, our lovemaking was conducted rather gingerly. That was something else that was new to me – sex before marriage. My folks would not approve. Based on all the scriptures that came to mind, neither would God. But in spite of their disapproval, Becky and I connected and began spending more time together.

And Becky started noticing my humdrum life. She worked as a waitress at Country Roads, a combination family-style restaurant and gift shop capitalizing on a somewhat romanticized version of the Colorado lifestyle, and on the old John Denver song. The fact that his song had been about the Blue Ridge Mountains of West Virginia apparently escaped their notice.

When we would share with each other what our days had been like, she noticed that her days as a waitress at Country Roads, while similar, still varied to some extent. My customary comment about my day was, "same as usual," or "nothing out of the ordinary." She used to say that it was okay, as long as I was happy.

But now, I got the feeling that she wasn't entirely sure that I *was* happy.

My job that afternoon, in support of Becky's lament, was much like my morning. Quitting time was 2:00, when the next shift took over.

I retraced my route from the morning and, despite the heavier afternoon traffic, was home before 3:00. I put my lunch bag on the kitchen counter and got a short tumbler from the cabinet. I mixed a quick Manhattan, then went into the living room where I settled into my favorite chair. I took a sip and pulled my phone out of my pocket. The only number in my favorites list was Becky. I touched her ID picture and then the green telephone receiver icon. I took another sip as I listened to the rings.

"Hi, Jack," she answered. Her voice sounded tired. Or maybe frustrated?

"Hi, babe," I replied. "I missed you this morning."

"I'm sorry. I just couldn't sleep and decided I'd probably be more comfortable in my own bed."

"Are you sure you weren't just mad at me?"

"No, Jack," she sighed, "I'm not mad at you. And I'm sorry I sounded like that last night. I've been thinking about it, and I don't have any right to get upset at you just because I don't think your life is exciting or varied enough."

"Well, I thought some of what you said made perfect sense, though," I conceded.

"Only some of it?" I smiled as I heard Becky snicker quietly. "Seriously, though, if you're okay with the way your life goes, it's none of my business."

"Well, it could be."

"It could be what?"

"If we end up wanting to be a permanent part of each other's lives, you may have to get used to hearing that my day was just like the one before."

"Are you asking me to marry you?"

"Well, no. Not yet. But, I mean – I really like you, honey. In fact – I uh, I think I love you. And I'm starting to think that maybe, someday – well, we might – " I felt as if my tongue was dragging on the ground and I was tripping over it. Thankfully, Becky rescued me.

"Relax, Jack," she interrupted. "Why don't we just wait and see how it plays out, okay? You might decide that my crazy, breakneck life is just too much for you."

I smiled and made a soft scoffing sound.

"Really, though," Becky continued, "*are* you okay with your life as it is?"

As I thought about my answer, I started feeling a little uncomfortable again.

"I admit there are some things I'd change if I could. But you're the part of my life that I like the best."

"Well, that's nice," Becky replied a little hesitantly, "and don't get me wrong, I'm flattered by that. But I really think you should be happy with your own life before you try to bring somebody else into it."

"Well, if I thought my life was already so great, why would I *want* anybody else in it?"

"I'm not saying it should be perfect. And there's nothing wrong with wanting someone else in your life. The point is that you need to be complete on your own. Expecting someone else to complete you is too great a burden to put on them."

"I see what you mean," I said. "And I *am* generally happy with my life. You're the one who doesn't seem that happy with it." I heard Becky sigh.

"Like I said earlier, I don't have any right to make personal judgments about your life. But listen, Jack, I'm just about to leave for work. Maybe we can meet for dinner tomorrow night and talk a little more."

"That sounds good, Becky. I really do want you in my life."

After disconnecting, I sat there for a few minutes, feeling a little better than I had all day. Maybe there was hope for us after all.

The leaves fluttered in the light breeze as long shadows lay across the ground at the feet of the trees. The sun was warm, but the shade and the early autumn breeze made the air deceptively cool.

The front door of the simple little white clapboard cottage at 112 Mercer Street opened and a man emerged. Moving with the deliberate slowness of age, he pulled the door closed, then looked around from the vantage point of his porch. Satisfied with what he saw, he clamped his pipe between his teeth and carefully went down the four steps, then out the front gate.

The man was a familiar sight in the neighborhood, but while he had a ready smile for anyone he met on the way, he didn't stop to engage in conversation. The breeze caught his neglected silvery hair, blowing it in all directions, but he didn't seem to notice. He fumbled with the top button of his tweed overcoat, keeping it tight around his neck, as he continued southwest on Mercer.

He seemed lost in his thoughts, but those familiar with him were aware that he was very much in control and knew exactly where he was in relation to his musings. Still, though, he gave little thought to his attire. His trousers, a little baggy for his frame, looked as if he might have slept in them. And with each step, his bare ankles could be seen, as he saw no need for socks.

The breeze caught the pipe smoke trailing behind him and whisked it away, as another puff from his mouth replaced it. He rounded the corner onto Olden Lane, and he paused at a trash can as the large headline on the front of the New York Times lying on top caught his eye:

JAPAN SURRENDERS TO ALLIES, TRUMAN SETS TODAY AS V-J DAY

It was yesterday's paper, and he had already heard the news. Still, the headline held his attention. As he stared at it, a slight smile played about his lips beneath the bushy mustache, but there was a tired sadness in his eyes as he recalled the part he himself had played.

He took another puff on his pipe but, realizing that the tobacco was depleted and the fire out, he tapped the pipe on the edge of the trash can a couple of times, then slipped it into his coat pocket. He continued on his way and, eventually, the brick Georgian-style edifice of Fuld Hall, the headquarters of the Institute for Advanced Study, came into view.

Completed six years before, in 1939, the building stood less than two miles away from Princeton University. However, the IAS was an independent institution, and was the academic home of numerous scientific luminaries of the time.

He continued past the trees dotting the park in front of the building, anxious to get to his office where he could refill his pipe. People were coming and going, some smiling at him, but he kept moving, his head down a bit, as he continued resolutely toward the front of the building. He pulled the white door open and went inside.

As he approached Room 115, he saw that his secretary, Helen, was already there. She was on the phone, so he just smiled and nodded as he passed her, and stepped into his office. As he closed the door, he looked down the length of the long room and saw a young man turn toward him from the bay window. He squinted at him as he couldn't recognize him, backlit as he was in front of the window.

"Dr. Einstein," the young man greeted him, "good morning."

18

"Ah, Dr. Curtis," Albert said as he recognized the voice, his pronunciation slow and precise, bathed in a thick German accent. "You have me in your debt. I am afraid I can never repay the number of visits you have paid me."

"That's not a problem, sir," Curtis said with a smile. "I was just hoping I could have a few words with you about your bridge idea, before your day began."

"My boy, I apologize, but I believe I've already said all I know on the subject."

Curtis laughed as if he had just heard a joke.

"Nonsense, sir. You're the leading mind on the topic."

"That was a long time ago, son. And I must share the credit for that particular theory with Dr. Nathan Rosen."

"Oh, of course, I understand that, Dr. Einstein. And I admit I wouldn't mind talking to Dr. Rosen as well, but since he's now teaching at the University of North Carolina, it probably won't be today." Curtis smiled at him again.

Albert sighed quietly and motioned toward the chairs in front of the desk. He unbuttoned his coat and pulled it off, hanging it on a hook, retrieving his pipe from the pocket. The tired look was in his eyes again, but as that expression, to an extent, was a common component of his features, the young man didn't seem to notice.

As Curtis sat down before him, Albert settled himself behind his messy desk, reaching for his tobacco. He took a moment to stuff the bowl of the pipe, then struck a match, puffing the tobacco to life. Feeling fortified, he looked up at Curtis and smiled.

The alarm tones had barely been quieted on my phone, and I was up and out of bed. I felt better this morning than I had the day before, feeling as if I had made a little progress in my relationship with Becky yesterday afternoon. In my typical elaborate bed-making routine, I flipped the covers up over the pillows.

I turned the thermostat up and started the coffee. I got cleaned up and dressed, poured my first cup of coffee and made my lunch. As I looked in the pantry where I kept the cereal, I decided this morning on Honey Nut Cheerios. And no, not just because it was Friday.

According to schedule, I finished up my cereal and my coffee. I brushed my teeth, pulled on a coat, gathered up my lunch and keys, and I left, pulling the door hard. I started up the car and pulled out of the circular driveway onto the county road.

The sky was clear, and being away from the city lights, there was a riot of stars overhead, and a gorgeous full moon. I felt a little more inclined this morning to notice them. Something about being on good terms with Becky just made me more observant of the natural beauty around me. While there hadn't been any major developments with regard to our relationship, I was looking forward to dinner with her tonight. And I was encouraged by her apology and her desire to work things out with me.

I was taking another glance up at the moon, and had slowed down a bit, when I was nearly hit by another car coming up behind me. I swerved to the right, onto the shoulder, as the car sped past. I hadn't even seen the car coming until it was practically on my bumper, and it continued on its way as if nothing had happened.

"Asshole!" I shouted as I pulled back onto the road, as if he could have heard me. But even as I said it, I was squinting ahead at the offending vehicle. There was something very odd about it. Starlight was illuminating it to some extent, but it was still too dark to see details from this distance. I pressed the accelerator pedal. I had to get closer.

As I gained on the car, I could see an old Plymouth Fury, with a mismatched rear fender panel taken from a different Fury.

"What are the chances of that?" I mumbled under my breath. I got closer to the car and squinted. My headlights didn't seem to be doing much. But I noticed the license plate. The number was the same as mine.

How could that be? A duplicate license plate, on an identical car? I stomped the gas pedal to the floor. My old car sputtered and groaned a bit, and managed a couple more miles per hour. Now only a few feet behind the duplicate, I was in the other lane on the two lane road, thankful that there was no other traffic coming.

I was nearly beside the car now, when suddenly it vanished, as if it simply drove through a shimmery curtain. It happened so quickly, I couldn't be certain of what I saw. But at fifty miles an hour, it seemed as if a green-colored light traced the contour of the car from front to back, swallowing it whole, and it was gone.

In a panic, I hit the brakes, my tires screeching to a stop, and I looked around. I sat there, panting as if I had just run to this spot instead of driving.

I cautiously pulled off the road onto the shoulder, and I got out. The winter air was cold, and I zipped up my coat. I walked back to the spot on the road where the car had disappeared. I wasn't sure what I was looking for. Some sign that it had been there? Some indication of whatever cataclysmic event had taken it away?

But there was nothing. At least as far as the Milky Way and the full moon would illuminate, there were no skid marks except for my own. There was no smell of smoke or any other burned substance. Only a stretch of county road, forsaken except for myself and my old idling Plymouth Fury.

I looked off the road, making a mental note of my location, based on a clump of large, old cottonwood trees, flanked by a couple of blue spruce.

Despite the lack of any physical evidence of what had transpired, I continued wandering around the area. I was seeking, as the scripture admonished, but I just wasn't finding. There had to be something. Some proof that I wasn't going completely bonkers.

After searching for several minutes and not finding any further confirmation, though, I wasn't so sure.

I got to work a couple of minutes late, and as you might imagine, I had a really hard time focusing on my job. While it didn't require a great deal of concentration, Rob, my supervisor, caught a couple of errors I had made, when the printed packing list didn't match the order.

The first time was no big deal. I opened the cartons and corrected the discrepancy. The second time in a couple of hours, though, Rob was concerned.

"Here's another one, Jack," he said as he held up the order and the copy of the packing list. I compared them and immediately saw the problem.

"Sorry, Rob," I sighed. "I'll fix it."

"Is something wrong?" Rob asked. "This isn't like you."

I looked at him, pondering for a few seconds. I was on good terms with Rob. I wouldn't really consider him a friend, but somebody I could confide in.

Not about this, though, I finally decided. Nobody would believe me.

"No, I'm just tired," I replied with a shake of my head. "Sorry, I'll take care of this."

"Okay. Well, I'm here if you need to talk."

I nodded and Rob turned and walked away. The good and caring management was one of the reasons that I had been happy to stay at this job for so long. I took pride in my work, and these mistakes, and Rob's kindness and understanding, were just plain embarrassing.

I managed to get through the rest of the morning without any further mistakes, and I spent my lunch time eating with one hand and browsing my phone with the other.

Maybe somebody else had experienced something similar. Maybe they had proof and were able to report it to somebody who might actually believe them.

But I couldn't find anything in local or regional news that resembled what I had witnessed. From there, I checked national and international news, but my search was fruitless. By the time my lunch break was over, I was even more frustrated than before. But I had to focus my mind on my work. I couldn't make any more mistakes.

Two o'clock finally arrived, and as usual, I was anxious to leave. I wasn't as anxious to get home, though. When I arrived at the cottonwood and spruce trees that I had noted early in the morning, I pulled over and got out of my car. The sun was shining brightly and, while it was still chilly, it was much more comfortable than it had been in the morning. I hoped that seeing the area in the full light of day would be more revealing.

My hopes were dashed within a matter of seconds. There seriously wasn't any sign whatsoever that anything out of the ordinary had happened here, other than the marks my own tires had made when I went off the road onto the shoulder. How could something of that magnitude happen without leaving any evidence?

Even though there was nothing to see, that didn't stop me from wandering around there like an idiot for at least a half hour looking for something, anything to prove to myself that I wasn't going crazy.

From there, I went home and did an even more thorough online search on my computer. I found no references to anything that sounded like what I had witnessed.

Maybe I *was* going crazy.

I resolved that I wasn't going to tell Becky about it at dinner. I didn't want *her* thinking I was crazy, too.

But she knew something was up.

"You're really quiet, tonight," she said.

"I'm *always* quiet. That's what you like about me." I smiled, hoping it would make me seem lighthearted. Which I definitely wasn't.

"Well, you're quieter than usual. I don't think you've said ten words so far this evening."

That wasn't entirely accurate. I had said more than ten words when ordering my beer and dinner at Mama Leña's, a Mexican restaurant we both liked in Northglenn. And I had just said nine words in response to her observation as we sat there at our table. But I knew what she meant, and I didn't want to be a smartass to her.

"I just have a lot on my mind," I finally said.

"Anything I can help with?"

I looked at her for a few seconds. Part of me wanted someone I knew and respected to tell me that I'm not crazy for seeing what I thought I saw. But to open myself up to that possibility, I would have to tell her what I thought I saw, and I knew how crazy it really sounded.

"No, I don't think so," I replied. I saw what looked like disappointment in her eyes. "It's nothing, really."

"You know," she said, "if this relationship is going to have any chance of working, you're going to have to let me be a part of your life. I know you like your routines, and I'm coming to terms with that. But you've made a routine of dealing with everything by yourself."

"Some things I *have* to take care of myself."

"I know, and I understand that. But that doesn't mean you can't let me in. Share with me."

She put her hand on mine as she looked at me. I was tempted, but her impression of my sanity, however false it may be at this point, was still important to me.

"I will." I turned my hand over and closed it around hers. "I promise." She looked at me a bit longer. Finally, she seemed to be resigned to the fact that it wouldn't be tonight, and she nodded slightly.

"You look really nice," I said, trying to soften the blow of my not sharing my worries with her. "I like your hair. What's that called?"

"It's a French twist," she smiled. "And don't think I didn't notice that you changed the subject."

I smiled sheepishly back at her.

"I just think it looks pretty. I like it. It's fancier than your usual braid."

"Thank you, Jack."

My not so successful attempt to change the subject was aided and abetted by the waitress when she brought our food. Mama Leña's made great chile rellenos, nice and crispy, smothered with lots of cheese and a delicious green chile sauce.

Needless to say, I now had a good excuse to be quiet.

Until Becky spoke up again.

"So, how was work today?"

Her question brought back the stress of the day, and I sighed before I looked up and saw the half smile on her face. It was only then that I realized that she was making a joke about the sameness of my days. She heard the sigh, though, and I saw her smile vaporize as she understood, again, that I wasn't telling her everything.

"It was just a tough day," I said, trying to minimize it, as I pushed the green chile around my plate.

I glanced up at her again and saw her studying my face.

"Are you worried about something, Jack?" she asked. "Are you worried about us?"

"No," I insisted. "Honey, we're the one thing I'm truly happy with in my life. I just need to get used to making you a regular part of it."

She seemed somewhat appeased by that.

"Okay," she said with a slightly hesitant tone of voice. "Well, I'm here anytime you need an ear or a shoulder."

"Thank you, Becky. I appreciate that. I really do." She offered her hand across the table again, and I took it. "And I promise you," I continued, "I'll take you up on your offer and make use of both of those body parts."

"Just those two?" A bit of a sly smile slipped back onto her face.

"And others, whenever they're offered." I smiled back at her. Coming from that conservative Christian farming background, I had never been one to employ sexual innuendo. Donna, my ex-wife, had been of that same conservative ilk as well, so this was something a little new to me. And yes, I know that my response was quite mild, but still, talking openly and joking around about sex gave me a little thrill.

With all those scriptures about sexual immorality and obscene joking, God probably wasn't so amused.

As dinner progressed, we relaxed after that initial tension.

"I'm going to visit my dad tomorrow," Becky told me. "Would you like to come along and meet him?"

Her mom had died when Becky was young, but her dad was pretty old now and lived in an assisted-living facility. That kind of place always gave me the willies, but I was touched that she felt ready for me to meet the family.

"I'd love to," I replied. The way her face brightened up at that made me almost want to spill my guts about the other thing.

Almost.

"He's been kind of anxious to meet you," she said. "I've been with you longer than any other guy I've been with since my divorce from Tommy, and Dad's starting to realize that you may be someone special."

I gave her hand a little squeeze.

"He sounds like a fascinating person," I replied. "He worked for NOAA, didn't he?"

"Most recently," she nodded. "He worked in various atmospheric and meteorological laboratories through the years in Denver and Boulder when I was growing up. Then, when NOAA consolidated those labs, he helped set up the Skaggs Research Center in Boulder in the late 80s, and he had his own laboratory there until he retired."

"I'm looking forward to meeting him."

I really was. Because a notion had appeared in my head. I didn't know if it would be feasible or not. But what might *he* say about the weird happening I had witnessed? Would a scientist completely unspoiled by the prejudice of religion be open-minded to something of that nature? Would he offer possibilities and explanations? Or, with that scientific background, would he be more likely to recommend a *specific* facility for me to be remanded to, for treatment of my obvious mental disability?

It was still in the back of my mind when I pulled up in front of Becky's house. Though she had been brought up in the country, she now lived in a split-level built in the eighties, in one of those suburban neighborhoods that abhorred straight streets and city blocks.

"Do you want to come in?" she asked. "I work the breakfast shift tomorrow, so I have to leave early. But you're welcome to spend the night."

I smiled as, once again, I felt that guilty thrill.

"I'd love to."

We meandered up to her door, and I held the storm door open as she slipped her key in the lock. Once inside, out of the sight of the neighbors, Becky placed her purse and keys on the table by the door, then she turned to me. She leaned against me and tilted her head back, and I kissed her. It was a sweet and tender kiss, gradually turning more passionate.

My feelings, as I had so adroitly expressed on the phone yesterday afternoon, had deepened over time. More and more, I was feeling the stirrings of love for this pretty lady. And it gave me a warm feeling to know that those feelings were being returned.

I caressed her back as our kiss continued, pulling her tightly against me. Tasting her tongue in my mouth, feeling her breasts pressed against my chest, I began experiencing a growing sensation down below, which Becky also pressed against. Finally, she pushed away from me and pulled me by the hands. Her eyes were full of desire as she led me to the stairs.

I climbed the steps, counting the various scriptures that came to mind condemning passion and fornication.

The lecture hall at Princeton was full, and the sea of mostly young faces looked up at Albert, many of the heads cocked to the side a bit, straining to catch his words through the accent. He took a moment to look at a few of the faces as he wrapped up his speech.

"Racism is a disease which is eating up America. An infectious disease of startling and genetic virulence, being passed from one generation to the next. But, like a biological disease, there is a treatment, and organizations like the National Association for the Advancement of Colored People," he motioned toward the pair of representatives sitting behind him, "are doing what they can to administer the vaccine. We must work with them to eradicate this nasty disease."

As Albert stepped back a bit from the podium, the audience erupted in applause. He gave a slight, bashful nod in lieu of a bow, but he moved back toward the podium when a hand went up.

"Yes?" he asked, acknowledging the student.

"Dr. Einstein," the young woman said after the applause had died down, "don't you think you're being a little excessive in saying that racism is eating up America? There's a branch here in Princeton of the national association that you're promoting today. There's Lincoln University that has been granting college degrees to colored people for years. Isn't that proof that racism is losing ground in America?"

"That might seem to be the case at first glance," Albert said. "And these organizations are to be commended for the fine work they do. But they have their hands full. By themselves, they cannot fight the scourge of racism. It's up to each of us as individuals all working together. We all need to act like white blood cells and attack the disease and fight it, driving it from the body of this country."

"So, besides a physicist, you're also a biologist?" laughed a young man.

"It would seem so, yes," Albert smiled.

"Dr. Einstein," another young man said, "it's rumored that you paid the tuition for a colored student who couldn't afford to pay. Is that true?"

"Hmm," he fidgeted, "I had not heard that rumor." He quickly pointed to another hand, hoping nobody noticed that he hadn't answered the question.

"Dr. Einstein, you believe that gravity is not a force from within a body in space. Rather, the body warps space, like a ball resting on a stretched fabric. Another body is drawn to the ball, not because of the weight or mass of the ball, but because of the warp of the space around it, correct?" Albert peered through the sea of faces, finally finding the speaker.

"Dr. Curtis," he replied, "I am here to speak about the scourge of racism, not about my past discoveries in physics and mathematics."

"I understand, sir, but I'm just wondering if you have had any success in manipulating and making use of that warp in space."

"My boy," Albert sighed, "as I have told you in the past, I'm a theoretical physicist. I deal in mathematical models and abstractions. Experimental physics is a different branch of study altogether."

"That's what I meant," Curtis persisted. "Have you created any models that demonstrated or made use of the warping of space?"

"If there are no other questions," Albert said, turning his attention back to the audience, "then we will adjourn." A couple of other hands went up at that point, but Albert had already turned away from the podium. He shook hands with the NAACP representatives, then made his way offstage.

He was in the hallway when he felt a hand on his arm, and he turned to see Dr. Curtis beside him.

"Hey, Professor," he said with a sly smile, "why are you giving me the brush off?"

"Dr. Curtis," Albert said tiredly, "I've answered your questions to the best of my ability. I'm afraid I can't tell you anymore than I already have."

"I know, but I've still got a few other questions that I was hoping you could answer."

"That was all a long time ago, young man. I'm happy now in my quiet hibernation at the IAS. I'm not one to keep reliving old discoveries."

"I'm sorry to keep bugging you about it. But I just find it fascinating, and I think I'd like to do some experimentation with some of your work."

"Well, you're certainly welcome to do that, my boy. Perhaps you should spend some time in the library. I've published a number of papers on the topics you've inquired about."

"Yeah, maybe I will," Curtis said good-naturedly. "I'm really sorry I've bothered you so much."

Seeing the look on Curtis' face, the old man felt a little regret at his dismissal of him.

"Maybe you could look up Dr. Edgar Lowenbaum, in the physics department here in Princeton. He's an engineer and has done some experimentation with a few of my theories."

Curtis' face lit up at that, and Albert felt a little better.

"I sure will, sir!" Curtis enthused. "Thank you so much."

"Good day, son."

Albert turned and shuffled down the hallway, toward the exit.

Becky didn't usually do the early morning shift, but when she did, if I was around, it really didn't cause much of a disruption. Country Roads opened at six o'clock in the morning, and Becky didn't take very long to get ready. Since I usually woke up early whether I had to work or not, I was usually awake before her alarm went off at four-thirty.

But I liked lying there, watching her get out of bed all "nekkid and purty."

As she started getting dressed, I got up and made her bed. She liked her bed *actually* made, so I spent more time on it than I did on my own bed. When I spent the night with Becky, my morning routines went out the window. And oddly enough, I was perfectly okay with that.

"I should be home by 3:30," she said as she worked her hair back into her trademark braid. "We can leave from here to go to the nursing home to visit my dad."

"Sounds good, babe," I replied as I replaced the throw pillows she kept on her bed. "I'll be here."

Not wanting to get in her way as she rushed around getting ready, I said goodbye to her and left at 5:00. Early Saturday morning traffic was considerably lighter than on weekdays, and I was soon heading north on the county road that leads to my house.

I saw headlights coming toward me, probably a local farmer heading into town for supplies.

I realized that I was wrong when the car passed me. As it continued on its way south, I saw that it was the old Plymouth Fury I had seen yesterday, the one with the mismatched fender panels, and my license plate. I hit the brakes and turned around, speeding after the vehicle, my mind racing as I tried to figure out how an apparently identical car with identical license plates could exist.

That's what was occupying my mind at the moment, not the way the car had gotten away from me yesterday. Almost as if I didn't accept that the vehicle had just vanished through a curtain of green-colored sparks.

That is until it happened again. I hadn't gotten as close this morning, and the bogey was still several yards ahead, when again, I saw a flash of shimmery green and the car simply disappeared.

But I had the same reaction. I screeched to a stop, panting as if I had just run a marathon. I looked around and realized that, to the best of my discernment, it had happened at exactly the same location. I saw the stand of cottonwoods flanked by the two spruce trees.

After I had duplicated yesterday's fruitless and frustrating search for proof beyond what I thought I had seen with my own eyes, I turned around and went home.

I perused the internet for a while, searching for different variations of the description of the visible effect that I had seen. I tried to think of as many different ways to describe it as I could. But again, using all the search terms I could call to mind, there was nothing at all in the news.

If it was an entirely localized event, and the locality was my county road in rural Weld County, Colorado at 5:11 in the morning, then it's no wonder I'm the only one who had seen it. It did occur to me that I could bring somebody with me, maybe Becky, in the hopes that, if it should happen again, she would see it, too. But the fact was that I was already becoming dubious about my own sanity. I didn't want to endanger it in her mind as well.

At 10:00, I headed for the library. I figured that I could browse the shelves for a while, looking for things like "duplicate license plates," "disappearing cars" and "green sparks." Assuming that I had comparable luck at the library as I had online, then my second line of attack would be to ask a librarian.

At least I didn't know them personally, so I figured that their looks of derision and disparagement might not make as deep an impression.

As it turned out, I had bad news, and more bad news: First, I was right about the first part. I couldn't find anything that fit the description of what I had witnessed. Not even on the more benign topic of duplicate cars and license plates.

Secondly, their looks *did* make an impression. I started out by asking about it hypothetically.

"I'm a writer," I said when one of the librarians was available. "I'm working on a science fiction novel, and I have this scene in my head. There's a car speeding down the road, and it suddenly disappears through a shimmering curtain of green sparks. I'm wondering if there might be any kind of phenomenon in real life that could give that effect."

She looked at me for a few seconds, the look on her face not quite scrutable. Finally, her face moved, but not in a very encouraging way. Her eyebrows came together as if she couldn't figure me out.

"Don't you have it backwards?" she asked.

"What do you mean?"

"Well, you're telling a story. You're describing a specific event. You've said what happens to the car, at least from the reader's point of view. But what *really* happens to it? Where does it go? What are you trying to accomplish in describing this event? That's the main thing to consider in the story. What it

38

looks like would be secondary, and as the author, it can look any way you want it to."

"Yeah, I know," I stumbled. "But I just have this specific image in my head. Really detailed. I want to use it, but I want it to be realistic."

"I'm sorry, maybe I'm not understanding you. It's science fiction, right? A car vanishes into thin air. Realism doesn't seem like the main consideration here."

I looked at her for a bit. She looked back at me. It might have been considered a standoff if there were any real stakes involved. Finally, I sighed.

"Okay, here's the thing: I'm not a novelist. I'm not writing a science fiction story. I actually saw this happen. Two days in a row, yesterday and today. I know it's crazy. Believe me, I know it can't be real, and yet I saw it. Twice! I have to find out what happened. What could cause that?"

Her eyes narrowed as she sized me up. Probably wondering if she needed to call security. I didn't even know if the library *had* a security force, but I kept expecting to feel iron hands close around my arms as two burly guys in black escorted me out.

"No," she finally said, "I don't know of anything in real life that could do that." Her tone made it clear that she was finished with me.

I looked at her for a moment, pondering whether I should press the issue. Ultimately, I nodded and muttered thanks to her. I walked out, wondering if I could ever show my face in there again.

I went back home feeling defeated. I couldn't believe that there was absolutely nothing that could explain what I had seen. But I guess that, for everything that *has* been documented, it had to start somewhere. Somebody had to be the first to see it.

As far as duplicate cars, disappearing in a blaze of green sparks, I guess I was the first.

I searched around and found a spiral-bound notebook. There were a couple of pages of writing at the beginning, but glancing over them, I saw that it was old and nothing that needed to be saved. I tore them out. If I was the first to see this, it was up to me to document it.

I started making a list:

      Plymouth Fury like mine, same mismatched fender panels

      License plate same number as mine

      Both sightings (Friday, Saturday) at 5:11 am

It turned out to be a pretty short list. For some reason, it was surprising to me how agitated and upset I was about something I knew so little about.

But then, it was a duplicate of my car, my license plate. I knew identity theft was a big problem. What kind of trouble could this person be making for me? Were there traffic violations being piled up on my record?

What if he was a bank robber and used that car as the getaway vehicle? What if people were killed in the commission of the crimes? Granted, my car was not a likely candidate for a getaway car, but still, would the police come knocking at my door to haul me off to jail?

I felt as if I was getting paranoid. Yet at the same time, an actual duplicate of my car and license plate seemed to me to be a pretty good reason to be concerned, don't you think? But you can't fight something you don't know anything about. That you can't even find.

I felt powerless.

"Dad, this is Jack Hobbes," Becky said. "Jack, my dad, Bill Barlow."

"Nice to meet you, sir," I said as I shook his hand. It was cool and particularly smooth, and felt quite fragile. It's hard to tell how tall he was. He was in a wheelchair, and kind of twisted around a little, but he had the look of an old geek.

"I'm happy to meet you, son," he replied as he shoved his glasses up on his nose. They immediately slid back down.

"So, you both have comic book character names," I said, laughing a little nervously.

"What do you mean?"

"Like Peter Parker, Lois Lane, Bruce Banner. A lot of comic book characters have alliterative names." He looked at me with a somewhat blank expression.

"My name is William," he finally said.

"Yes, sir," I replied meekly. "Sorry." I glanced up at Becky, but she just smiled and rolled her eyes.

"Knock it off, Dad," she said. "Don't intimidate my boyfriend."

I looked back at him and saw a slightly twisted smile playing about his mouth.

"Well, sit down, sit down," he said, motioning toward the old threadbare sofa. The place smelled like most old folks' homes. A combination of must, an accumulation of food smells from the last several meals, and that general but hard-to-describe smell that old people have.

Becky and I sat down, and as Becky kept up an exchange with him about how he's been doing since the last time she was there, I looked around. There was a dresser topped with a number of photographs in frames, some of them ornate and gilded. A few were old family photos, a couple of which I had seen copies of at Becky's place. Others seemed more professional, like line-ups of scientists celebrating discoveries or something like that.

I still didn't know how I was going to talk to him about my crazy early morning visions without Becky hearing, but a few minutes into their conversation, the answer appeared on its own.

"You're out of your blood-pressure medicine?" Becky asked. Her voice was more irritated than alarmed.

"I took the last one yesterday," he replied. "The refill is ready at Walgreens."

"Well, I wish you'd told me. I could have picked it up on the way here."

"Sorry, I forgot about it."

Becky sighed, picked up her purse and looked at me.

"You want to come?" she asked. "I'll just be a few minutes."

"I'll stay and keep him company," I replied.

It seemed as if she liked my answer. I wondered how she would feel if she knew my reason.

"Okay, I'll be right back." She gave me a quick peck and then she left.

"So," I said, hoping to make the best use of what little time I might have, "I understand you worked for NOAA."

"Yes, I did," he said, his face perking up a bit.

"What sort of work did you do?"

"I did loads of research. Really boring shit." I shook my head a little and smiled when I could see that he was jabbing me again. He shifted and resettled himself in his wheelchair. "I created some weather models that are still being used by some meteorologists today," he continued. "Let's see, I designed a couple of systems for a weather satellite."

I didn't really want to hear his entire work history, but what I had heard so far didn't seem like anything that would be able to explain a disappearing car. Still, his qualifications were better than mine.

"I need a little help with something," I blurted out, plowing through my misgivings. "I'm hoping that somebody with a scientific background might be able to give me some insight. I've witnessed something that I can't explain, and it's driving me crazy."

Mr. Barlow's eyes brightened up a little, and I wondered how often he was given a mental challenge.

"Let's hear it," he said with a smile.

I told him about seeing the duplicate of my car, and how in both instances, it had vanished in a curtain of green sparks. He looked at me for a while after I finished relating the story, and I tried to figure out how my sanity was faring in his scientific mind. Finally, he spoke.

"Very curious," he said. "And you weren't snockered?"

"I'm sorry?"

"Potted. Sloshed. Plastered. Tipsy. Had you been drinking?"

"Oh, no sir. I was on my way to work yesterday, and this morning, I saw it on my way home from Becky's house."

"After a night of debauchery with my daughter, huh?"

"Uh – " I felt a nervous flutter in my stomach until I saw that smile on his face again.

"Your physical description of the phenomenon kind of reminds me of the aurora borealis," he said, ignoring my discomfiture.

"The northern lights?"

"Yes, that's right. Although, as the name implies, they're never seen this far south. Also, they're always up in the sky. It's an atmospheric phenomenon. They're never seen at ground level. And probably most importantly, they aren't known to eat cars."

"You don't believe me, do you?"

"Son," he said placatingly, "I've seen a lot of weird shit in my life. A lot of it couldn't be explained very easily, but eventually, it was. Some of it *still* hasn't been explained, but that doesn't make it any less real. So when you tell me you saw a car drive into a ground-level aurora borealis and disappear, I see two possibilities. One, you're the first to witness an unusual phenomenon that has yet to be explained. And believe me, every phenomenon that has ever been witnessed by man had to have a first witness, so that in itself isn't that unusual."

"I was kind of thinking something along those lines myself earlier," I responded. "You said you saw two possibilities. What's the second one?"

"That you're a whacko."

"I've been starting to think that, too."

He looked at me over his glasses which had slid down again.

"Well, my little girl's got a pretty good head on her shoulders. She gets that from me, you know. And I've had problems with some of her gentleman callers in the past, but none of them have been loonies. So I'm more inclined to go with the first possibility."

"That's good to know."

"What does Becky think about this?"

"Actually," I said, squirming a little, "I haven't told her about it. I don't want *her* thinking I'm nuts."

"Hmm. Well, like I said, she's got a pretty good head on her shoulders. And if she thinks as much of you as she seems to, I tend to think that her estimate of you won't change too much."

I wasn't quite so sure, but it sounded good.

"Thank you, sir. I'll think about it."

"Sorry I couldn't be any more help than I was."

"Actually, even though you couldn't explain it, I still feel better about it, knowing that I'm not necessarily going crazy."

"Well, that was just one of the possibilities. We'll see how it plays out." I smiled at him again, but this time, he just looked back at me blankly. "What?" he asked, but he couldn't hold the serious expression for very long. "Would you like something to drink?" he asked with a smile.

"Sure, that'd be nice," I replied. "But I can get it."

"I know you can," he said gruffly. "The booze cabinet's over there." I stood up and walked over to the cabinet that he had indicated.

"Would you like anything?" I asked.

"You know how to make a Manhattan?"

"My favorite. Yes, I do."

"Have a few of those, maybe you'll see your vanishing car on the way home."

The telephone on Albert's desk rang, a long, sustained bell. He calmly reached over and picked up the receiver.

"Hello?"

"What did I ever do to you?" The voice was familiar. And irritated.

"Excuse me?"

"Why did you send that eager beaver scientist after me?"

"Ah, Edgar," Albert said with a chuckle and a warm smile. "I'm sorry, my friend. Dr. Curtis can be a bit overwhelming, but he means well."

"Yeah, well your Dr. Ronald Curtis cost me a whole afternoon. The kid doesn't know when to let go."

"Were you able to help him?"

"I answered a few of his questions, but when he kept at it, well, I admit I got a little angry. I told him I didn't have time. It didn't matter, though. He wanted to know about experiments I had done based on your theories."

"Which ones?"

"All of them! He was especially focused on your ideas about warping space and time, and your bridge theory. But once I told him I hadn't done any work with them, then he kept pressing me about everything I've done related to your work. I finally told him if he doesn't lay off, I'd warp his skull."

Albert smiled.

"I honestly hoped that you might be able to tell him about what he was wanting to know. Me, I'm just a theoretical

physicist. I think up ideas. They're just theories, calculations. You're the one working in applied science."

"Yeah, well I'm sorry I got upset," Lowenbaum said. "It just seemed like he was giving me the third degree." He sighed. "Friend of yours?"

"Not so much a friend as an acquaintance. He's a relative of Professor Curtis, there in Princeton. He's come around the IAS a few times wanting to know more about my work. I admit his attention is a little flattering. I just didn't know what else to tell him. He's a nice boy, very bright, and he's got an enthusiasm that, I admit, makes me feel a little nostalgic."

"Hmm. Yeah, now that you mention it, I guess he kind of reminds me of myself some years back, too. I'll tell you what: I'll give a little thought to some of the work I've done based on your calculations, and if I come up with anything that I think he might be interested in, I'll give you a call."

"Thank you, Edgar. You're a good man."

"Yeah, well . . ."

Sunday had been nice. Becky spent the night at my place. She didn't have to work, so we slept late, made love, had a leisurely breakfast, watched a movie, made love again. It was a good day.

Aside from that occasional feeling of guilt about the "sexual immorality." I had to get past that.

Maybe I just needed more practice.

Monday, as usual, came too soon. On Sunday, Becky was enough of a distraction that I had pretty much forgotten about the case of the auto borealis. But Monday, it was on my mind again.

I carried out my morning routine quickly, and I got on the road a little earlier than usual. I had never seen where the "DupliCar" had come from, only where it disappeared. So I went to an intersection of two county roads, a mile or so before the car vanished on both occasions.

And I waited.

I waited until I couldn't wait any longer. There was nothing but dark, and I was going to be late to work.

Tuesday I had similar enthusiasm, although it was tempered a little by the disappointment I had felt the day before. This time, though, I saw it!

I was facing south, idling just off the road, when I saw a green flash over my left shoulder. I shifted into drive, and as the car sped past, I pulled onto the road behind it, accelerating to catch up.

I examined the car and, again, was amazed at how much it looked like mine. And of course, there was the license plate.

Seeing no oncoming traffic, I pulled into the northbound lane and sped up. I wanted to get a look at who was driving "my" car. He seemed oblivious as I pulled up even with him.

There are some things that I don't think a person can prepare themselves for. Expect the unexpected? How does one even do that?

Well, I just about had a heart attack when I looked over at him and saw, illuminated by his dashboard lights, my own face! It was me driving the car beside me!

I started feeling lightheaded and realized that I was holding my breath. I blew it out, but without thinking, sucked another breath into my lungs just as quickly.

He (I?) never turned to look at me. I was about to have a meltdown, but he apparently wasn't affected at all. Me? I couldn't turn away. I was incredulous. I was fascinated. I was terrified! Now, *I* was the one who was oblivious.

Because I didn't notice the northbound car coming toward me in the lane I was driving in. I was snapped out of my delirium when I heard his horn blaring. I looked up into blinding headlights. I heard the oncoming car's tires screeching on the pavement and the immediacy of what was about to happen to me finally ripped my attention away from my doppelganger. I noticed that the oncoming car was fishtailing out of control.

I hit the brakes, swerving to the left onto the shoulder, trying to keep my car pointed forward as I skidded. The other me in the DupliCar never slowed at all.

All that I could tell about the oncoming vehicle was that it was a red newer model car. Struggling for control, it was turned diagonally and skidding right toward me. I could see the passenger side door heading toward my car, his headlights shining across the road toward the other me in the DupliCar.

Suddenly, his tires regained traction with the pavement. However, since he was pointing toward the other me, while I was ecstatic to see that he wasn't sliding toward me any longer, I was disheartened to see that he now swerved directly into the path of the other Fury.

In that split second that I saw what was happening, I steeled myself for a horrendous head-on collision. For the ear-splitting crash, the rending of metal, the shattering of glass.

Instead, the cars went right through each other.

Think for a second about what I just said. That other me, driving the DupliCar, continued on his merry way, passing directly through the red car as if it wasn't even there.

And disappeared in a curtain of green sparks.

I realized at that moment that I was panting for breath. My knuckles were white, my hands aching from gripping the steering wheel. My heart was pounding so hard that I was sure it must be getting bruised against my ribs.

My neck muscles resisted as I turned my head to see the red car. It was stopped a few yards behind me, but then it took off, smoke spreading out from its spinning tires. I could only imagine the panic that driver was feeling, but I was happy to see him go. While it was reassuring in a way for someone else to have seen what I had been witnessing, still I didn't feel as if I would have been able to interact with him in any coherent way.

I turned back and looked at where the DupliCar had vanished. I thought about what I had just seen. I knew it couldn't have really happened, and yet I had seen it happen!

You know, I did pretty well in school. I especially enjoyed science, to the chagrin of my devout Christian fundamentalist parents. I knew that one solid object can't just pass through another one. I knew that, unlike the atoms of a gas or a liquid, the atoms of solid elements are fixed, arranged in such a way that makes the object rigid. A solid doesn't pass through another solid without inflicting some damage on one or both.

So how does one deal with witnessing the impossible? All your life, you see the aftermath of enough traffic accidents to know that one car can't just pass through another. Yet I had just seen that very thing happen. How do you reconcile something you see with your very own eyes with the science that it contradicts?

Just ahead of me, off the side of the road, I saw the big stand of cottonwood trees and the two spruce.

I drifted through my morning at work giving little thought to what I was doing. To my knowledge, I didn't make any mistakes. At least, Rob never brought any discrepancies to my attention. But I was happy when lunch time arrived.

The first thing I checked on my phone was the news. But nothing had been reported about the phantom Fury. The driver of the red car was probably as hesitant to report something crazy like that as I had been.

After that, I got out the notebook that I had started on Saturday and made some new entries.

> Duplicate car driven by ME!
> No substance - other car passed <u>right through</u>
> <u>it!</u>

I thought for a while, then decided that I needed to enter the more mundane details. I noted that I had not been out on Sunday, so I didn't know if "JackSimile" made an appearance. I also noted that he definitely did not appear on Monday.

As I was writing, somebody entered the lunch room. I self-consciously closed the notebook as I looked up. It was Annie, a salesperson from the front office. I didn't know her that well, but she was a nice lady. Kind of plump with a ready smile. I had been to her house for the Christmas party she and her husband threw last month.

She had apparently noticed my surreptitiously closing the notebook, because she smiled slyly at me.

"Watcha writing?" she asked.

"Nothing," I said in an attempted nonchalance. Even I thought I failed pretty miserably.

Annie looked at me with a disbelieving look on her face, and though she obviously wanted to know what I was doing, she didn't press it. She just continued toward the coffee maker. But then I felt bad, because I knew she knew I was lying.

I had gotten along pretty well with her and her husband, Bob, and like the librarian, since I didn't really know her that well, I decided to take a chance.

"Okay," I said, "here's the thing. You can't tell *anybody* what I'm about to tell you, alright?"

Her face brightened and, her coffee forgotten, she came to my table for whatever juicy tidbit I was about to share with her.

"Friday morning, and then again on Saturday morning, I saw a car exactly like mine." Somebody seeing a car similar to their own wasn't that unusual, but the face she made told me that she remembered *my* car. "That car also had my license plate."

She screwed up her face in confusion.

"I don't get it. Somebody copied your car?"

"Well, no. Not exactly. I saw it again this morning, and I was able to get up beside it, and it was me driving. I saw *myself* in the driver's seat of this duplicate."

I could see her eyes squinting a bit as she tried to determine my agenda.

"Then," I continued, "another car almost hit me, but instead, drove right through that duplicate as if it wasn't even there."

"Okay," she said, a knowing look on her face now, "you're just messing with me."

"Swear to God," I said, raising my right hand as if I was taking an oath. "It's as if the duplicate car was made of air. Like it was a ghost."

Annie stared at me for a few moments until she started shaking her head.

"Jack, are you dabbling in the occult?"

"The occult? No, I'm not dabbling in anything. I'm just telling you what I saw."

"You didn't just see it. You were *in* it."

"I know. That's what I'm saying. It was weird."

"You need to get yourself back to church, Jack," she said. I had forgotten that she was a born-again Christian. "That sounds like the works of the devil! You get away from God, you make room for Satan's evil tricks!"

"Well, I don't think it's Satan, Annie," I said, trying to choose my words carefully. I didn't want to get into a religious discussion with her. "I just think it's some kind of phenomenon that we don't know anything about yet." I was grateful for the discussion I had had with Becky's dad on Saturday.

"Oh, really?" Annie said cynically. "Like what?"

I frowned at her.

"If we don't know anything about it yet, how would I know?" Then, suddenly, an idea popped into my head, thanks to a number of science fiction stories I had read. "Maybe a different dimension. A parallel universe."

Annie sighed through her nose and shook her head again, her face wearing a scornful look.

"Typical non-believer," she sighed, "spouting your science-y mumbo-jumbo, trying to make the unnatural and godless sound perfectly natural."

"I'm sorry I bothered you with this, Annie." I started gathering up my things. "I need to get back to work."

"Yeah, well you need to get back to Jesus, too. You're not going to get to heaven by cavorting with demons."

"Okay, thanks. I appreciate your thoughts." The last I saw of her as I left the lunch room, she was still shaking her head, likely praying for my soul.

Becky had to work that night, so I was left to my own devices. Normally, my evening would consist of eating dinner, usually something really simple when it was just me, and watching something on TV.

This evening, though, I had a lot on my mind. Primarily the new ideas that had entered my head during the discussion with Annie at lunch.

I spent hours searching the internet for pages about additional dimensions beyond the three we're familiar with, or four if you count time. I couldn't understand a lot of it, but the possibilities the theory opened up were fascinating.

I also found a lot of information about multiple universes – or multiverses – which I freely admit was also pretty much over my head.

Some scientists argued against the theory of multiple universes, not because they could prove that they didn't exist, but precisely because it *couldn't* be proven. Belief in it required, they said, not so much a scientific approach, but an act of faith.

Since I was already experiencing something of a crisis of faith, maybe that theory wasn't for me. On the other hand, perhaps what I had witnessed was the proof that had been lacking up until now.

At any rate, I forgot to eat and, before I knew it, it was way past my bed time. For someone who gets up at four in the morning, that's a big deal.

I grabbed a muffin from my fridge and ate it to keep the hunger pains at bay long enough to get to sleep. My sacred routines were imperiled.

I went to bed thinking I'd be doing well to get five hours of sleep.

"I've made some blunders in my life," Albert said shaking his head, his eyes a little teary. He looked at his friend sitting across from him in his office. "But perhaps the worst was signing that awful letter to President Roosevelt."

In 1939, a group of Hungarian scientists living in the United States, headed by Leo Szilard, had attempted to warn Washington about the Germans' atomic bomb research, but their warning was discounted. At Szilard's urging, Einstein added his name to a renewed warning, and suggested that America begin its own nuclear weapons research. As a pacifist, this went against Albert's own beliefs and position, but knowing that Hitler would have no qualms about using the bomb if the Germans were successful, he thought it might be a good idea, as a deterrent.

With Einstein's name attached to it, Roosevelt listened. Thus began the Manhattan Project. Now, just six years later, two atomic bombs had been exploded over Japan, vaporizing over a hundred thousand people. Over the course of three days, they proved once and for all the deadly accuracy of Albert's relativity theory, particularly the incredible amount of energy stored in the tiny mass of the nucleus of an atom.

"I know it went against your principles," Albert's friend and fellow scientist Linus Pauling replied, "but it seemed necessary at the time."

"Yes, it did. And now, thousands of innocent people are gone forever."

"It could have been a lot worse."

"It is a lot worse! Have you seen the news? Have you seen what's happening to the survivors? They're little more than rotting corpses who just haven't fallen down yet."

Linus inclined his head and sighed.

"Yes, I'm afraid I have seen that." He looked up at Albert. "Ava's urging me to do something, to use my influence, which I think she overestimates."

"I know your wife is a pacifist, too," Albert said with a nod. "What does she want you to do?"

"I don't know. I'm not sure what I can do. I believe she thinks I'm more important than I am."

Albert smiled and took a couple of thoughtful puffs on his pipe.

"I've given a few talks back home in California," Linus continued, "but I don't know how effective I've been. Ava has told me I don't seem convincing. I've talked about the science of the bomb, but apparently I haven't done as well in talking about the human cost."

"I've been thinking about something myself," Albert said, pondering the swirling cloud of smoke. Linus watched him, and waited. "You're right, the people need to be warned about the dangers of nuclear weapons. America won the war, but we're still making more weapons."

"Don't they already know? It seems obvious, having seen what happened in Japan."

"Yes, but now America is working on developing a hydrogen bomb, much more powerful than the two bombs they dropped on Japan."

"More powerful?" Linus said shaking his head. "I wish nuclear fission had never been discovered."

"Ah, but it could also be very useful," Albert said, perking up a bit, "in a peaceful setting. Szilard patented the idea of a *nuclear reactor in '39, and I think it could be beneficial for producing power for homes across the country."*

Linus was thoughtful.

"Hmm. Nuclear energy generated in a peaceful setting, yes, I can see how that could be a good thing. Education about that would certainly be helpful." Albert could see the wheels start turning in Linus' brain. "An enormous amount of energy could be generated from a relatively small amount of fuel. 'The energy of the future.'"

Both men smiled at each other. Linus glanced at his wristwatch, and he sat forward quickly. "I need to go. I have a train to catch."

"Thank you for visiting, my friend," Albert said.

"It was my pleasure, as always. Let me know if you come up with anything about your idea, about warning the public. I think I might like to get involved. And I know Ava would like that."

"I certainly will," Albert nodded as both men rose. Albert, still puffing his pipe, followed behind Linus, and stopped as he pulled on his coat.

Turning to look at Albert, Linus put out his hand. Albert smiled and shook it.

"It was good to see you, Albert," Linus said. Then, sharpening his gaze into Albert's eyes, he leaned closer. "And please don't spend too much time feeling bad about that letter. You're a good man. We all make mistakes." Albert raised his eyebrows a bit, thinking about the cost of his mistake in human lives, but he didn't say anything. "But I'm not even sure that was a mistake, given the circumstances."

"Thank you, Linus."

Wednesday was different. I know that, considering what I've been relating, that statement might seem a little redundant. But it was even different in the context of my recent observations, because I made a big discovery.

It started out the same, beginning with my usual – though rushed – morning routines at home. I got out to where I had waited yesterday morning, except that I parked a little farther back. Since the other me in the Phantom Fury had appeared behind me yesterday morning, I gave myself a little more room to be able to see his entrance.

Yesterday, I had started thinking of the other me as JackSimile, simply because it was easier to refer to "him" as a different person, instead of "the other me." Besides, I thought it sounded kind of cool.

I was idling and in gear, my foot on the brake, when the green flash occurred right beside me. I took off, accelerating as quickly as my old car would let me. Even as I gained on JackSimile, I was studying the car for any other clues.

And I found one. I was close, and again, I noticed that my headlights didn't seem to have any effect on the car ahead of me. The car appeared solid, but I knew from my previous close call that it had no substance. Was that why my headlights wouldn't illuminate it?

But I was looking at the license plate, and I noticed the stickers on it. I had bought the car, way back when, in December, so the sticker on the left had a "12" on it. The year sticker, on the right, said "18." I knew that the year sticker on "my" plate said "17" and would expire eleven months from now.

I was seeing myself at some point in the future!

I couldn't tell how far in the future. December of 2018 was nearly two years ahead of me, and my current tag wouldn't expire for almost another year. So it could be anytime in 2018.

I carefully pulled to the left in the northbound lane, determined to keep a close eye on any potential oncoming traffic. But I had spent a little too long behind the car looking at the license plate. I had just come up even with JackSimile when we reached the stand of cottonwood trees and he vanished through that curtain of green sparks.

So I had my answer. It was time travel. Or rather, "time viewing," since I wasn't actually entering a different time, but simply getting a glimpse of it.

I had no idea why or how, though. What could cause such a phenomenon? Why did it involve me?

At lunch, I made a note in my notebook of the new piece of information I had gained this morning.

Tags expire December 2018 – FUTURE ME!

It was only one point, but what a big deal it was! I was able to see into the future! Granted, all I could see was me driving my car, something I do every morning. I admit it would have been especially cool to see something of major historical significance taking place.

But I couldn't deny that seeing myself in the future was pretty cool, too!

Each day that week, I waited in my usual spot, and I took off after JackSimile, noting every detail I could find. But Friday, I got confused.

Everything started out the same as the other times. I accelerated, coming up beside the Phantom Fury, but this time, there was something different.

My car had begun its life nearly four decades ago as a metallic gold. The front right fender panel had to be replaced a few years ago when rust ate all the way through the lower portion of it and it broke away from the chassis. When I drove, I was told, the lower part of the panel would flap in the wind. So I found one from a junk yard and replaced it. It was green.

I performed a similar replacement on the left rear panel two years ago. It was now grey.

Except the left rear panel on the Phantom Fury was still rusted gold. Puzzled, I slowed down a bit so I could see the license plate. The year sticker said "14."

What the hell?

We reached the cottonwoods and the car vanished, leaving me completely befuddled.

The latest entry in my notebook was made with trepidation. I didn't know what to make of it. Granted, before this, I didn't exactly have it all figured out, either. I didn't know why I was seeing into the future, or how. But I had come to accept it.

But now, everything was different. This time, I didn't see into the future, but into the past. What had happened? Why the change? I had no idea.

When I noted my observation of the rear fender panel, I also made note of the current date, and of the fact that this glimpse was at sometime in 2014.

I saw Annie once again that week, but she kept her distance.

I had made a decision about Becky. With all of this documentation of multiple sightings, I decided I was going to tell her about JackSimile and the Phantom Fury.

She came to my place for dinner on Friday. I could see immediately that she seemed tense. I gave her a glass of wine and went back to assembling the salad. It wasn't that hard, since they started packaging ready-made salads. I just had to divide it all up into two separate bowls.

I looked at Becky as she took a sip of wine. I took a breath, building up my nerve. But she spoke first.

"So," she said, "I hear you're seeing disappearing cars?"

Dammit!

"Becky, I was just about to tell you all about it." Apparently, I couldn't think and make salads at the same time, so I stopped and turned toward her.

"Well, I heard it from my dad."

"He wasn't supposed to say anything."

"He's old. He forgets. So, why didn't you want me to know about it?"

"Because I know how crazy it sounds." I walked toward her, maintaining eye contact. "I care about you, Becky. I care about what you think of me. I didn't want you thinking I was flipping out."

"Are you?"

"No!" I insisted, gesturing wildly. "That's just it. That's why I was going to tell you about it now. I've been documenting everything that I've seen." I picked up my notebook from the counter. "I've got it figured out. I mean, I figured out what's happening. Not the why or the how."

I handed Becky the notebook, and she took it from me hesitantly. She put her wine glass down on the counter, and she held my gaze for a few moments before she finally opened the notebook. I watched her face as she read the entries. As she read,

64

I noticed that her expression never changed. Finally, she looked up at me.

"Jack, this is crazy."

"I thought so, too," I replied, "until I *kept* seeing it. Always in exactly the same place and time."

"How does that make it less crazy?"

"I don't know," I said, shaking my head in frustration. "Other than the fact that it's not an isolated occurrence. It's repeated, even predictable."

"It's becoming a routine, and you're finding a certain comfort in that."

I stopped and thought about that for a second.

"Huh. Maybe so."

She stared at me for a few moments, and I forced myself to keep quiet and wait for her to speak. When she finally did, it wasn't too encouraging.

"Just because it's becoming a routine doesn't make it any less crazy. Or worrisome."

"It also doesn't make it any less real."

"You're talking science fiction, Jack!"

"Probably most modern science was science fiction just a few decades ago." I put my hands on her shoulders. "Honey, you know me. You know how much I'm settled in my routines. Knowing that alone, why would I make up something like this?"

"I didn't say you were making it up."

"You know I'm not crazy."

"Not usually," she said as her expression softened just a bit.

"Why don't you come with me tomorrow?" I asked. "You can see for yourself."

"Even without the duplicates, that sounds crazy." I could tell by her tone that I was winning her over. "You want us to get up early on a Saturday, when neither of us have to work, so we can be on the road at," she glanced back down at the notebook, "5:11

65

a.m., so we can watch a car driven by you in the future as it appears and disappears into thin air?"

"Well, Becky, when you say it like that, of course it sounds crazy."

She smiled ever so slightly. I took her in my arms and she snuggled up against me, the side of her face against my chest, and she sighed.

Probably wondering how long until I actually went over the edge.

We were in position by 5:05. We had six minutes to wait, and during that time, neither of us said a word. I was tense, excited. Becky was right: this *had* become a routine, and it was one that fascinated me.

I think Becky was quiet mainly because she was tired, and possibly nervous about my state of mind. But I was just too nervous and excited to speak.

I kept a close eye on the analog clock in my instrument panel. Naturally, it was just creeping. The minute hand slowly swept past the 2. When it showed 5:11, I stepped on the brake and put the car in gear.

At 5:12, I started feeling confused, and a little irritated. At 5:13, I looked over at Becky, who was already looking at me. I couldn't tell what she was thinking. Illuminated by the dashboard lights, she didn't really look irritated, but to be honest, I couldn't read her expression.

"I don't understand," I said quietly, my voice dripping with disappointment. "I saw it *last* Saturday, on the way home from your place. I was sure I'd see it again today."

"Why don't we just go back home and get some rest?" she said in a soft, soothing voice. That voice made me angry, as if she felt she had to try to keep me calm.

"I'm not crazy, Becky."

"I didn't say you were." That soft, 'don't go crazy' voice continued to irritate me. I forced myself to not respond. I knew if I did, I'd regret it.

We drove quietly back to my house where we both managed to continue the silence, staying out of each other's way.

Finally, Becky decided to go back to her place. She said she had some things she needed to do before she went to work in the afternoon. I was irritated enough that I didn't mind.

After she left, I threw myself down on the sofa and opened my notebook, resentfully noting that JackSimile and the Phantom Fury didn't bother to show up today.

He did show up the next day, though. Naturally, I was alone, so my sanity had to remain in question in Becky's mind.

There was something noteworthy about this sighting. *Really* fucking noteworthy!

I know, I just made God frown with that language. But what happened this time practically deserved its own notebook!

I saw more than just my future self. There was another car that came up behind him and passed. What made it even more noteworthy was the fact that, in once again paying such close attention to details relating to the Phantom Fury, I didn't notice the car coming up behind us.

I didn't notice it until it was inside *my own* car!

Remember how the Phantom Fury passed through that red car a few days ago? Well, this car passed through mine as if it was a ghost.

I had been leaning forward, peering at details of the back of JackSimile's car, so the headlights coming up behind me in the rear view mirror escaped my notice. But when the headlights passed through my trunk and my back seat and then through the front seat and shone on my dashboard, I gotta admit that was a little difficult to miss! (My mind was a little busy at the time, but

I thought later that it was a little weird that his headlights illuminated me and my car, but not the other way around.)

I looked down and saw the front grill of a blue Honda Accord. I knew it was an Accord, because I recognized it as Jim Greggor's car. Jim was my neighbor, about half a mile north.

I struggled not to panic! I mean, just try to imagine this: You're looking down and seeing the front of another car, not only passing through your car, but *through your own body!*

Holy shit!

I saw the hood of Jim's car cutting right through my belly. Granted, I couldn't feel it, but I could just imagine what would be happening to my man parts and my legs if they passed through the fan blades and other moving parts of an internal combustion engine in *my own* time. All that shit going on under the hood was, fortunately, not felt by me, but just the thought of it *really* gave me the willies!

A couple of seconds later, I saw the interior of Jim's car. Along with my own dashboard, I saw his much newer and nicer dashboard. I saw his steering wheel with his hands positioned at ten and two.

What was even creepier was when, as the car was getting ready to pass, *Jim himself actually passed through me!* We were occupying the same space, but in different times!

He pulled into the left lane and passed JackSimile, waving at him as he did, although it didn't look as if JackSimile waved back. Then, Jim continued on his way.

All of this took only a few seconds, and they both vanished in green sparks at the cottonwoods.

But it left me shivering with the heebie-freaking-jeebies for the rest of the day!

"You'll be alright?" Adele Gödel asked as she and Kurt were leaving.

"Yes, of course," Albert said with a smile. "It's been nine years."

"I know, but still . . ."

"I'm fine, Adele. Thank you."

It was December 20, the ninth anniversary of Elsa's death. Albert and Elsa Einstein were cousins, and their marriage had been somewhat novel. They were never considered great lovers, but they were good companions. They shared a similar sense of humor and understood each other. They never had any children together, but were quite happy in each other's company.

She had died after a painful illness a year after they had bought the house. Her death had been hard on Albert, and he had immersed himself in his work to distract himself.

"I'll see you tomorrow," Kurt said, shaking Albert's hand.

"Yes, my friend," Albert said. "Thank you both." It had been Adele's idea to take Albert for an evening out, to make the anniversary easier. While neither of the men had seen the point of her concern, it had been an enjoyable evening.

Adele and Kurt were both from Austria and had fled the Nazi takeover of their home, but they were an unlikely couple. Adele was a pretty, outgoing divorcee, a former cabaret dancer, while Kurt was thin and quiet, with occasional bouts of depression and paranoia. He was also six years her junior. His religious parents had been against the union, but they were devoted to each other.

Albert and Kurt were unlikely friends, as well. Albert, who gave little thought to his appearance, often seemed rumpled and disheveled, while Kurt, twenty-seven years younger than Albert, usually looked dapper in a suit and tie. And socks. Albert relied heavily on mathematics and the laws of physics. Kurt, while a mathematician, was also a philosopher. They differed politically, religiously, and in other areas, but they were good friends and lived near each other. Albert was known to say that his own work at the IAS was of little consequence, and that he only worked there for the walks home with Kurt.

He closed the door after Kurt and Adele left and, too stimulated to sleep, went into his study and sat down. Albert had loved music all his life. He had once said that "if I were not a physicist, I would probably be a musician. I often think in music. I live my daydreams in music. I see my life in terms of music... I get most joy in life out of music."

Adele's idea for the evening had been to take Albert to listen to a local woodwinds ensemble. Albert had fallen deeply in love with Mozart's music at an early age, and enjoyed playing his sonatas on his violin. Tonight, though, there were no violins. They had played Mozart's Serenade No.10 in B-Flat Major, a serenade composed for wind instruments, and they did a lovely job.

The first two movements were played with skill and feeling. At the beginning of the third movement, though, the Adagio, Albert was transfixed. Though he wasn't aware of it at the time, he had stiffened up a little. Adele had noticed, and had nudged Kurt, asking him to see if Albert was alright.

It had taken a couple of pokes for Kurt to be able to get through to Albert, but Albert assured him that he was fine. When he had come up with his theory of relativity so long ago, he had withdrawn for about two weeks, completely immersed in his thoughts and notes. Tonight, for the sake of his friends, he had exercised a supreme effort and got his attention back on the music, saving his other thoughts for later.

Thinking back on it now, Albert remembered the opening of the Adagio. It was a simple beginning, a pulsing tempo played by bassoons and basset horns. Then, the oboe came in, playing a long, sustained note high above the tempo. That sustained high B was what made Albert sit forward, no longer paying attention to the music.

It was probably all those visits he had received from Dr. Curtis during the previous months that had his mind on some of his earlier works. And when that sustained B was playing, it was as if something clicked into place.

That note, long and unwavering, could be the key to an old issue.

For the next couple of weeks, this became my morning routine. Up early, even on the weekend, and out on the road by a little after five. Follow JackSimile and the Phantom Fury until they drove through the curtain of green sparks, then to work or back home to enter information in the notebook about each particular sighting.

There were some days when "he" didn't show up, and I documented those days, as well. I couldn't see any pattern to it. It seemed random, but then I admit that I don't really have a very analytical mind.

I made up again with Becky. Sort of. She still thought I was being a little weird, believing the crazy shit I had told her. She was also kind of hurt that I had decided to reveal it first to her father instead of to her. But I think I finally got her to see that the fact that he was a scientist made him the logical choice, in my mind at least, for a first revelation of something of this nature. She didn't bring it up again after that.

Annie, at work, seemed to be avoiding me. We didn't cross paths too often as it was, but the few times we came close to it, she acted as if she had forgotten something and turned around. Fine with me. With the cussing and the fornicating I had been doing lately, I felt like I was starting to get a handle on the guilt, so I didn't need her reviving it.

My job became little more than a distraction. I was able to keep my mind on my work enough to carry out my responsibilities without making too many errors. But all the time

73

I spent at SnakZone, felt like I was just killing time until I could get back home and focus on my new purpose.

I was still researching everything I could find about multiple dimensions and time travel and multiverses, both online and through library books. But it was difficult to learn anything definite since all the known science on the subjects was purely theoretical, and frequently contradictory.

Then, on a cold Saturday morning in February, everything changed.

The routine was the same as always. I was idling on the shoulder, foot on the brake, car in gear, when JackSimile flashed onto the road beside me. I started accelerating, preparing to pull into the northbound lane and come up beside him. When I saw headlights coming toward us, though, I waited, following behind him and, instead, studied the back of the car for any details I may have missed on previous viewings.

The headlights came closer, and I saw a small tanker truck with a big "FHG," the logo of Farm and Home Gas, plastered across the front of its tank. It was illuminated by either my headlights or the Phantom Fury's. I didn't know which, since I couldn't tell if the truck was in my time or JackSimile's.

But suddenly, I saw what looked like a puff of smoke in the cold morning air as one of the truck's tires blew. The truck skidded off the road, off the shoulder, and was headed toward a power pole. To avoid it, the driver turned back toward the road, but in trying to regain control, it looked as if he overcompensated. The truck bounced back up onto the asphalt, turning sideways across the road, although its momentum was still forward. Towards me!

It all happened fast, in just a couple of seconds, but in that time, I saw the truck tip and roll. JackSimile hit the brakes, and only then did I know that the truck was in the future. I stomped on the brakes, too, but I sailed right through the Phantom Fury.

Even though I knew the truck was only a spectral image from the future, I cringed as I saw it rolling over and over toward me. It bounced one last time on the top of its tank, and I screamed as I slid through it.

In that instant, the truck erupted in a brilliant blue fireball. I could almost feel the heat. Yes, I knew the explosion wouldn't occur for another year or so, but still, for a brief moment, I was seeing the blast from the inside!

As I came to a stop, I put my head back and took a deep breath, thankful that I had escaped injury and death so neatly. After a couple of seconds, though, that thought turned again to a feeling of panic. I turned my car around, and even though I knew that the burning wreckage was only an apparition, I went as far around it as I could, following the edge of the shoulder.

And as I came past it, I saw what I was afraid to see. Parts of the Phantom Fury were visible through the orange and blue flames, and the black billowing smoke. What was left of the truck was on top of the front half of the car.

My car.

In that moment, I knew how, and roughly when, I was going to die.

How can I express the feeling of having witnessed my own violent death?

I was in shock. I stood there at the crash site for several minutes, watching for movement, for any sign of life from either the car or the truck. But the only movement I could see was that of the flames and smoke engaged in their macabre dance.

I looked around me. On both sides of the road was farmland. The nearest house was maybe a mile away. It was early morning and dark. I didn't know how long it would take for somebody else to see the fire, and for them to call fire and rescue. Once called, I didn't know how long it would take for them to arrive, but I never saw anybody else approach.

Then, at 5:30, a brief green glow appeared around the wreckage. There was a shower of green sparks over the road, and the entire conflagration just vanished. There was no sign that anything had occurred there at all. No wreckage, no skid marks or scuffs on the road, not even the smell of smoke. No indication whatsoever of the lives that had ended so violently.

That *would* end so violently.

I pulled myself into my car, and I suddenly realized how tired and weak I felt. I just sat there for a few minutes, unable to move. The adrenaline rush of having been inside an explosion, followed by the realization that I was going to die in that explosion at some point in the fairly near future, left me with the strength and impetus of a damp rag.

I don't know how long I sat there. When I finally felt like I had the energy to move again, I started up my car and made my way back home.

I felt like a cancer patient who had just been told he had maybe a year to live. I felt dazed, sad, agitated, angry, depressed, and probably a few more feelings that I wasn't able to pick out. I spent most of the morning obsessively thinking about my upcoming death.

I thought about what JackSimile should have done at that fateful moment. Should he have sped up or slowed down? If he had hit the brakes at the moment of the truck's blowout, would that have saved him? The truck rolled a ways before coming to rest on top of the Phantom Fury and exploding. If the car hadn't been at that exact point, would the truck have continued rolling until it *did* come in contact with it?

If, on the other hand, JackSimile had kept up his speed, or even sped up, would he have gotten past the truck before it exploded? I just didn't know. And further, I didn't know which one he did, in order to judge the merits of choosing the other option.

And yes, I realize that I was still referring to JackSimile in the third person. It was a little easier to think objectively about the crash if *I* wasn't the one in the center of the fireball.

I wandered around my house, aimless, not knowing what to do with myself. After a while, I picked up my phone. I knew Becky had to work and was probably getting ready to go, but I decided I just wanted to hear her voice.

"Hi, Jack," she answered. "I can't talk long. I have to leave for work in a minute."

"I know," I replied quietly. "I just wanted to say hi."

"What's up?" she asked. Her voice had taken on a concerned quality. She could probably hear something in my voice.

"I know you think I'm nuts with this whole FutureView thing, and I just want you to know that I'm sorry I put you through that." I'm not sure why I had the urge to get that off my chest now. I still had at least a year.

There was a pause as Becky hesitated.

"That's okay, Jack," she finally said. Another pause as she seemed to cast about for what else to say. "Maybe I can go out with you another time and see it."

A little late for that.

"No," I replied. "There won't be another time. I saw myself die this morning."

She sighed, but didn't say anything.

"I know you don't believe what I saw," I continued, "and I don't blame you. I'm guessing you probably think I'm going over the edge now. But for what it's worth, at least I won't be bothering you about it anymore."

"I know *you* believe what you saw," she said diplomatically, "and I respect that. But whatever the cause, I'm glad it's behind you now. And I hope it stays there."

Kind of hard to ignore what was ahead, but I didn't say that.

"Anyway," I said, "I just wanted you to know."

"Are you alright?"

"Yeah, I am," I said, and I was a little surprised to realize that I really was. "I'd just like to see you. You want to come over after work?"

"Sure, if you like. I get off at seven."

"I can't wait to see you," I said. "I love you."

There was another pause, but then . . .

"I love you, too, Jack."

I don't think I had taken on a defeatist attitude. I *did* feel a little helpless in the face of my impending doom but, not knowing what to do about it, I think I decided to enjoy life to the extent possible.

Obvious things came to mind, of course. In fact, the first thing I thought of was to change my route to work, and I had pretty much already decided to do that. In my research, and in my reading of science fiction novels, I had learned that there were different schools of thought concerning changing history, even future history. For instance, if I changed my route, who's to say that I wouldn't die even sooner on my new route? Or, if I tried to change something, would "the universe" even let me?

But I was going to give it a shot.

Still, it had been pretty unnerving to see myself die a violent death, and I think that's what led to my "enjoy life to the fullest" attitude. It can all be taken away so quickly.

So when Becky arrived at 7:30, I met her at the door with a kiss and a hug and a glass of wine.

"Wow," she said with a smile, "what got into you?"

"Life," I replied. I thought for a moment about expanding on that, but I decided that that one word pretty much summed up my philosophy, so I left it at that.

I let go of her and she followed me into the kitchen where I had beef stroganoff simmering, which I knew was her favorite. She looked at me for a moment as she took a sip of wine. She seemed to be studying me.

"So," she finally said, a little hesitantly, "you saw yourself die this morning?"

"I did," I nodded, as I stirred the sauce. "But it's okay. We don't have to talk about it. In fact, I've already decided to change some routines to try to avoid it. For now, I just want to make sure I don't miss out on the good things."

I looked at Becky, still dressed in her uniform of white shirt, khaki-colored pants and burgundy apron. And I smiled.

She looked at me suspiciously.

"What?" she asked.

"I was just thinking that I've never undressed a waitress before." I looked her up and down seductively. Becky looked down at herself.

"You're actually turned on by this? This is one of the most *un*-sexy outfits I could be wearing."

"All the more reason to get it off of you."

"Oh my," she replied with a nervous flutter in her voice. She took a gulp of wine, then set her glass down on the counter as I came to her. She looked past my shoulder at the pan of sauce on the stove. "Do we have time for this?"

"Honey," I said, as I reached back and turned the burner off, "we have all the time in the world." I know, it was a little hokey, a little dramatic, but I didn't care.

When I took her in my arms, I kissed her lightly, brushing her lips softly with mine. She held me tightly as I started nibbling down her neck. Her body stiffened a little, but she pressed it tightly against me, and I took advantage of her close proximity to untie the strings on her Country Roads apron.

As she felt the apron loosen, she looked up at me, and her face displayed a passion I hadn't yet seen from her. I pulled the apron up and over her head and placed it on the counter. I looked down at her and it felt as if my heart grew a couple of sizes. It didn't matter a bit that she was wearing an unflattering pair of khaki pants and a basic white button front shirt. She was beautiful.

I unbuttoned her shirt and pushed it softly back from her shoulders. Becky put her arms down to her sides and let the shirt slide off onto the floor, but then, her hands were on me again. I brushed my lips across hers once more, and she grabbed me as if she was impatient for more. I kissed her lightly, but I made her wait for more than that.

I reached down and unfastened the khakis and pushed them down over her hips. As I felt the soft skin of her thighs, my desire grew to the point that I wanted to just grab her and rip the rest of her clothes off, but I held back. I took my time, slipping them past her calves. She stepped out of her shoes and the khakis, and I stood back up, taking in the sight.

Something about my look made tears gather in Becky's eyes. She smiled softly and, apparently now embracing my slow, "take my time" approach, she unbuttoned my own shirt, keeping her eyes on mine. She smiled at me, as a single tear slipped down her cheek. Knowing that the tear wasn't the result of unhappiness, I leaned forward and kissed it away, tasting its saltiness on my tongue.

At this time, it was as if the simmering desire in both of us had built to the boiling point. The passion was finally given free rein as our lips and tongues hungrily pressed against each other, our hands caressing each other's naked skin.

It had been years since I had done any farm work. My muscles weren't what they used to be, but I managed to sweep Becky up in my arms in a move that would do a movie hero proud. I carried her into my bedroom where we completed the task of undressing each other, and we made love tenderly, passionately, while our dinner got cold.

Albert sat peering at the blackboard in his office at the Institute for Advanced Study. On it were a number of scribbles, along with a few actual equations. But he wasn't getting anywhere with them. Part of the problem was that he didn't know where he wanted to go with them, or where they could go.

Thoughts and ideas had been swirling in his head recently, and he knew there were several contributing factors. A number of conversations he had recently engaged in had caused the initial itch of an idea to form.

Some of it was likely a result of his conversations in the past few months with Dr. Curtis, the young and persistent cousin of physics Professor Wendell Curtis, who taught at Princeton. Contributing to those thoughts were other conversations and occurrences. Talk about his past collaborations with Dr. Nathan Rosen. About Leo Szilard, the young Hungarian scientist who had convinced Albert to sign the letter to President Roosevelt about the atomic bomb. About Edgar Lowenbaum, the engineer at Princeton who had done a few experiments based on Albert's research, and to whom Albert had sent young Dr. Curtis with his questions.

Even that Mozart piece he had listened to with Kurt and Adele on the anniversary of Elsa's death.

It was all troubling, and he didn't know why. It used to come easier to him. He had made his initial mark in the world of physics when he was in his twenties. His revolutionary ideas on relativity, many of which have since been proven to be correct, had taken the world by storm.

Now, at nearly sixty-seven years old, his mind was still sharp, still visionary, but not as fast as it used to be. It took some pondering to see how all the pieces fit together. And to see which ones didn't fit at all. Glancing at the scattered notes on his desk, which had contributed to those on the blackboard, and vice versa, he wasn't sure if they even had anything to do with the problem, or if they were just random thoughts. Distractions.

Albert sighed. He turned toward his desk and picked up his pipe. He stuffed tobacco in the bowl, still regarding the markings on the blackboard. He scratched a match and lit the tobacco, squinting through the cloud of smoke.

He took one of the chairs in front of his desk and turned it toward the blackboard. Settling himself into it, he crossed his legs, puffed thoughtfully on the pipe, and examined what he had written.

A few minutes later, as the tobacco was giving its last, Albert felt as if he was no closer to figuring out what was bothering him. He just couldn't find where the itch was, so he couldn't scratch it.

He shook his head and sighed.

My relationship with Becky changed that night. True, we had determined before then that we were in love, and we had expressed those feelings in the bedroom. But that evening, our love gained a kind of freedom, an expressiveness that we hadn't allowed to possess us before. And that's actually the way it was. Our feelings weren't really ours anymore, but we were more possessed by our feelings.

Our love had taken us over, instead of the other way around.

In the days that followed, I continued my previous routine concerning driving to work. I knew I was safe on the old route since the accident wasn't to occur for another year or so. I just wanted to be completely sure about what I had seen.

And except for one day when that older version of JackSimile from 2014 appeared, he didn't show his face around these parts again.

February, aside from a couple of minor scattered snow days, had been fairly warm. By the time spring arrived, buds had already been poking out from the branches of trees, and the green tips of tulips and crocuses pushed up from the ground here and there.

One Saturday morning in May, on a rare occasion when I didn't wake up early, my bedroom was, not really flooded with sunlight, but just had a vaporous wash of morning filtering through the curtains.

Becky came into the room from the bathroom, walking in her sinuous, sensual way. Being naked, it was especially sexy and, as always, I appreciated the view. Her dark hair was longer when not pulled back in its braid, but it was still a little zig-zaggy. It draped across both sides of her face and over her shoulders, playing peek-a-boo with her nipples.

But she had a look on her face that I couldn't quite interpret.

She slid toward me and leaned down on her hands against the mattress, and I lifted the covers for her to rejoin me in bed. As she snuggled up against my body, she turned her face up to me, and it seemed her expression was one of nervous apprehension. I brushed the hair away from her face.

"What are you looking so mysterious about?" I asked, but I tried to soften the suspicious-sounding question with a smile.

She looked at me for a moment longer, as if wondering how to say whatever was on her mind. Finally, she apparently decided to come out with it.

"I'm pregnant," she said softly.

I think I looked at her a little stupidly for a couple of seconds until the news sank in. When it finally did, I could feel the smile spread across my face, and Becky's trepidation seemed to dissipate. I squeezed her and kissed her, and she wrapped her arms around me, but she pulled her face away enough to look in my eyes.

"You're not upset?" she asked.

"Aw, honey, why would I be upset? I love you. A child of our union is the perfect way to celebrate our love."

"But it's not an official union. You're okay with it even though we're not married?"

"Married or not, sweetheart, I love you and I'm fully committed to us."

Becky smiled at me and squirmed a little closer.

"You've become quite the heathen of late," she said.

"I know," I mused. "But honestly, I've realized that I don't care if we're married or not. I just know that I want to be with you for the rest of my life." Becky nuzzled against my neck and sighed. "Of course," I continued, "if you *wanted* to make it legal, I certainly wouldn't be against it."

She pulled her face away from my neck and looked at me. She smiled at me as she gazed into my eyes. Then, pressing her naked body tightly against mine, she kissed me in a very un-motherly fashion.

Becky and I got married in a quick and easy civil ceremony. Neither of us were religious, so we didn't feel the need for any kind of church service. But we both, it turned out, were comfortable enough with each other, and confident enough in our love, to make it official.

We discussed where we would live, and eventually, we decided that she would put her house up for sale. We both liked it, but it was smaller. Perfect for her, or even for a couple, but with a child, it would be a little cramped.

As is always the case, in the years that she had lived there, Becky had become comfortable and adjusted the house to her own lifestyle, giving it design touches and accent colors that suited her. But of course, to sell it, the house had to be made a little more generic. So the weeks that followed were busy as I helped her move her things out. Some came to my place, others were sold or donated.

"Time to get rid of my stuff, huh?" I asked one afternoon, half jokingly.

"Only if you want to," Becky replied.

"Really? You're not going to decide that my décor is too Neanderthal for you?" I was kidding, of course, but she looked at me seriously.

"Honey, I think it's extremely important that we each retain our own individuality. We're a couple, yes, but a couple is made up of two different people. We come together with a melding of styles, not just an adopting of one over the other."

I put my arm around her and smiled.

"Have I told you I love you?" I asked.

"A few times." She tilted her head back to receive the kiss that I felt impelled to plant on her lips.

"Well, I hope you don't get tired of hearing it."

"I think I can get used to it. But seriously, I'll never just assume that your stuff will have to go to make room for mine."

"Good to know."

"Fortunately," she grinned, "your stuff isn't *too* Neanderthal."

We did a thorough cleaning of her house, did some minor repairs inside and out, and then painted the interior. Her house was listed in the last week of June. It was a nice place, and it showed well. With the real estate market the way it was in the Denver area, it sold within the first week.

I stood in the doorway of what was now the nursery watching as Becky smoothed the bedding in the crib that I had just assembled. It was a little strange seeing the room that I had grown up in transformed into a baby's room. But it was perfect for it. It was a little small, and it was right next to the master bedroom.

We were way ahead of schedule. It was only July, and we already had many of the things we needed to prepare for the baby. We had also been investigating natural childbirth techniques and, under her doctor's supervision, began accumulating bits and pieces from various disciplines.

Becky was barely showing yet, but her body, already sensuously curvy, was just a little fuller, and she was wearing maternity wear, and looking really good in it.

She looked up at me and, despite the frequency of the adoring looks I gave her, she still smiled and shook her head.

"What now?" she asked.

"I'm just wondering how I ever got so lucky to have such a wise and wonderful woman in my life."

Her smile turned from the mock exasperation she had been displaying at my adoration to loving warmth as she came to me. I could just barely feel the growing tightness of her belly as it pressed against me.

"I'm pretty lucky myself," she said softly.

Without thinking, I made a disparaging face at that.

"What was that look for?" she asked.

"I don't know," I said, pondering how to answer. "I just feel like I'm kind of a mess."

"What are you talking about? You're a very sweet man with a nice home and a stable job."

"But I'm so big on routine. Spontaneity is not my strong suit."

"Nothing wrong with routines. And you can do spontaneity. I saw that with the whole JackSimile thing."

It had been a while since either of us had mentioned my FutureView episode.

"Yeah, I suppose. And I guess I did get away from my routines whenever I spent the night at your place."

"See? You're a mercurial and totally unpredictable bundle of capriciousness!"

"Mercurial capriciousness, huh?" I said, kissing her on the forehead. "Now you're just showing off."

She smiled up at me, and she turned to look back into the room. Everything was shaping up nicely, but when she turned back to face me, there seemed to be a little worry on her face.

"We're going to be good parents, aren't we, Jack?" she asked.

"Of course we are, honey," I said, pulling her closer. "How can you even doubt that? With your wisdom and beauty, and my stability and love of established routine, not to mention my prodigious abilities in assembling furniture," I motioned toward the crib, "we'll be a force to be reckoned with. We'll be the envy of other parents, and our child will become the standard by which other children in future generations will be measured."

"Oh God!" she retorted. "I hope not. Perfection is such a heavy mantle to bear."

"Nobody would know that better than you!"

She looked up at me, and the jokes slid away, leaving her face serious again.

"We've sure come a long way in the past year."

"Yes, we have," I agreed. "We were both so afraid to open up to another relationship. Now, I can't imagine *not* having you in my life."

As often happened in these moments of closeness, we ended up moving next door, to the master bedroom, where we were able to express how perfect we really were for each other.

Bill Barlow rolled his wheelchair backwards and looked up at us over his glasses as Becky and I came into his apartment. We had gone to visit him on a Saturday evening in July.

"How've you been doing, Dad?" Becky asked.

"Oh, you know," he said, "I'm a little tired from my run this morning, but other than that, I can't complain." Becky rolled her eyes. "How about you kids?" He motioned to the old threadbare sofa and we sat down.

"We're doing well," I said, smiling at his joke.

"Oh, well that's good," he said. "Now that you've impregnated my daughter, I'm glad you're able to feel good about your seminal prowess."

"Dad!" Becky sounded particularly exasperated.

He grinned and changed the subject.

"Would you like something to drink?"

"Sure," I said, getting up. "Manhattans?"

"Your fella sure has a thing for his alcohol, doesn't he?" he said in a confidential tone to Becky, but still loud enough that I would be sure to hear it. Then, he raised his voice. "Yes, son, I'll have a Manhattan."

He and Becky chatted while I made a couple of Manhattans and got a glass of seltzer for Becky. He thanked me as I handed him his glass, and I sat down on the sofa next to Becky and took a sip of my drink.

"Hey, I thought of you yesterday," Bill said looking at me. "I was reading in one of my journals about a couple of young local fellas trying to invent time travel."

"Really?" I replied, trying not to sound too interested. I had put all that behind me.

"Yeah, they've set up a lab up near where you live. They're calling their outfit ChronoLog. Maybe they can help keep you from dying next year."

"Thanks, but I think I have that under control. I'm taking a different route to work now."

"Oh," he said, "you think it's that easy to avoid your destiny, do you?"

"Well, if I'm not where the accident's going to happen, how can it kill me?"

"Son, when your time's up, how do you suppose you're just going to prevent it?"

"Since when are you such a fatalist?" Becky asked, and then I heard her exasperated exhalation when she saw the grin take its place on his face again.

"I'm just shitting you kids," he said. He reached over to the end table beside his wheelchair and picked up a magazine and handed it to me. "But here, just in case you ever want to get serious about cheating death."

The magazine, *Hypothesis*, showed a couple of grinning geeks, with the cover story, "Bridging the Gap from the Theoretical to the Practical." I leafed through the magazine briefly, just to be polite, then put it down on my lap and thanked him. I just didn't want to get caught up in that obsession again.

Don't get me wrong, it was still very much on my mind. And even though we hadn't talked about it, that wasn't because I didn't ever think about it. I mean you gotta admit that was some weird shit I witnessed. That's not something you can just purge from your mind. Maybe when I had an opportunity to myself, I'd have a look at the article.

But I knew that Becky didn't believe it had been real. Maybe that I had imagined it or something. I don't know. I just didn't want to bring back something that had left a bad taste in her mouth. So for her sake, I left it alone.

"I just thought," Bill continued, "you might be a little more concerned about not making my grandchild an orphan."

I could almost hear Becky's eyes roll.

Albert pulled his coat tightly around his neck against the cold. With the Christmas season in full swing, Kurt Gödel was busy with a holiday function of some kind. Kurt, while not a church-going man, was religious, a devout Christian. So this evening, Albert was making the walk home alone.

It was dark and a hard, grainy sleet was just beginning to blow around. Albert kept his head down, his white hair blowing wildly in the wind. Still, someone recognized him, a young woman with platinum blonde hair, swept to the side and down across one eye like Veronica Lake, although in the blustery weather, it wasn't staying in place very well.

"Professor Einstein," she gushed, "oh, my goodness, it's so exciting to meet you. Hey, listen, could you explain that theory of yours? Everybody's talking about it, but – "

"I'm sorry, miss," he interrupted. "People are always mistaking me for Professor Einstein." He smiled apologetically and continued on his way.

He didn't like the dishonesty, but it was a ruse he sometimes resorted to. Having become such a recognizable figure, even after all these years, strangers would stop him on the street and ask him to explain relativity to them. It didn't take many attempts to realize that it was not something that could easily be distilled into a twenty or thirty second answer, and it usually led to additional questions. So, in time, he had adopted the subterfuge. He wasn't sure if people actually believed it, or if it just threw them off balance long enough for him to make his getaway.

And it worked tonight. Ten minutes later, he was in his house and closed and locked the door. He struggled out of his heavy coat and hung it up, remembering to get the pipe from the pocket. He flipped on a couple of light switches as he made his way through the house, and he turned up the heat.

He went into the kitchen and looked in the refrigerator. Helen, his secretary and housekeeper, had left a casserole dish for him, ready to put in the oven. He clamped his pipe between his teeth and pulled the casserole out of the refrigerator. He slipped it into the oven, then struck a match to start it heating.

While his dinner cooked, he went to his study and sat down at his desk. His first task was to fill and light his pipe. Then, he opened a book that lay beside his telephone. Finding the correct page, he picked up the receiver and dialed a number, counting the rings.

"Hello?" came a voice over the distance.

"Good evening, my old friend," Albert said into the telephone. "It's good to hear your voice again."

"It's been a while," Nathan Rosen said, a bit of a Brooklyn accent coming through. "How are you?"

"I'm well, thank you. I'm still very happily collecting pay from the Institute of Advanced Study."

"The IAS is lucky to have you, Albert. I'm glad it's still such a good fit for you." There was an almost imperceptible change in his tone of voice as he changed the subject. "What's on your mind?"

Albert smiled. Not one for small talk himself, he liked the inclination of so many on the east coast to just get to the point.

"Actually, I have a number of things on my mind, but I haven't been able to focus them. I was thinking some outside perspectives might be helpful."

Becky had settled in very nicely in my house, and it quickly became our home. As she had said, she never arbitrarily determined that I should get rid of any of my stuff. When there was a question about anything, we discussed it and made the decision together. Thus, her things and my things blended into a nice, cohesive, homey décor.

At about six months now, she was showing quite a bit more. She had encountered some mood issues, which we discovered were not all that uncommon during pregnancy, but they were a little unnerving, when she would just break down crying. But we had also done many of the things that expecting couples usually did, including sharing the experience of feeling the baby kick. And we had engaged in a few discussions about baby names.

It had been determined that we were having a boy, so that made the discussions a little easier, although we still seemed to disagree on names.

"We are *not* naming our baby Calvin!" Becky had declared adamantly. She was looking in the baby name book she had recently purchased.

"Why not?" I demanded.

"Two reasons," she replied. "First of all, it means 'little bald one.'"

"Did you know that before you looked it up?"

"No, but that doesn't matter. He'll be able to look it up in the future just as easily as we did. I don't want him finding out we gave him such an unflattering name."

"Honey, Calvin is a celebrated name with quite a distinguished history," I said. "John Calvin was a well-known Protestant theologian."

"You're not religious anymore, so why do you care anything about that?"

"Well, I don't specifically, but . . ."

"And besides, that was his last name, not his given name."

"What about Calvin Coolidge?"

"What about him? Calvin was his middle name. His first name was John. Besides, I've never known you to care anything about political history, either, so why would you feel so strongly about him?"

I sighed, feeling my argument lose traction.

"You said there were two reasons."

"We are not naming our baby Calvin Hobbes!"

Damn! My favorite comic strip was the main reason I had begun considering the name Calvin. Becky was just too smart for me.

But then, I had known that for a while.

Since March, rather than driving south on my county road, I started turning onto the westbound road just south of my home, and working my way toward I-25. This way, I avoided the stretch of road where the accident I had witnessed occurred. (Would occur?)

In September, road construction crews set up operation on that east/west road, closing off the road in both directions from my county road. The detour kept me on my original southbound road.

Now, forced to drive on the doomed stretch of road, or drive a particularly long ways out of the way, I found myself taking an interest once again in my FutureView episode.

Becky had reduced her work hours, but she still did short, part-time shifts. The occasional mood swings could be challenging at times, and being on her feet for long periods of time was hard for her, but she actually enjoyed her work. She was one of those outgoing people who liked and got along well with others, and the interaction she had with customers of the restaurant was actually fun for her.

So, one evening while she was at work, I searched for and found the magazine that her dad had given me a couple of months before. *Hypothesis* was a profoundly scientific magazine with articles that were a few steps above my ability to really comprehend. The article about the two scientists on the front cover was no exception, and contained numerous diagrams and equations that made little or no sense to me. But if they had the ability to speak in simple English, they might be a good place to start.

One of them, Dr. Oren Bradley Curtis, was a theoretical physicist, and came from a whole family of scientists of various disciplines. A few of them had been fairly well celebrated, all the way back to Einstein's time. Curtis came from a moneyed background and had invested a chunk of his own fortune in the endeavor.

The other one, Dr. Josh Dunham, dealt in applied and experimental physics and had a more humble beginning but, through hard work and unexpected, out-of-the-box thinking, had made his own mark in the scientific community.

It turned out that they were quite close to my home. They had purchased a sizable plot of land about a mile east of me, and modified the house and outbuildings to carry out their experiments involving space-time. So, a couple of days later, when I knew Becky was going to be working the afternoon shift, and I wouldn't have to explain why I was late, I paid a visit to ChronoLog Laboratories on my way home from work.

It was an unassuming place. A rutted dirt driveway, much like any of the other driveways in the area, was marked by an old white mailbox with the hand-lettered word "ChronoLog" on the side. I drove past some scrubby-looking, naked elms, up to the white clapboard farmhouse and parked my rusty old Fury next to a couple of late-model cars. I almost expected to see a farm dog or two come running out to see who had pulled up, and maybe some chickens scratching in the dirt. But aside from the two cars, the place seemed empty and devoid of any activity.

I grabbed my JackSimile notebook and got out of my car, climbing the steps to the front porch. The place didn't have the look of a cutting-edge scientific laboratory at all. Instead, I could picture somebody like my mother, wearing a gingham dress and apron, opening the door, smiling as she wiped a smudge of flour from her face, and inviting me in for cookies, or maybe a Sunday dinner with the preacher.

That image was shattered, though, with the loud sound of the industrial-strength buzzer which sounded somewhere deep inside the house when I rang the bell.

Eventually, the door was opened by one of the two scientists I remembered from the cover of the magazine, Dr. Dunham. Several inches shorter than me, he appeared to be around thirty years old and bore no resemblance whatsoever to the image in my head of a scientist on the cutting edge of a new frontier. He was wearing a T-shirt with a graphic on it that said, "I frequently engage in full-frontal nerdity." His sandy-colored hair had kind of a ragged look to it, as if he was accustomed to keeping it in a shorter style, but was several weeks past when it should have been cut.

"Can I help you?" he asked. His voice was a little high-pitched and cracked as if puberty was coming late.

I realized belatedly that I hadn't really thought of what to say. Knowing that my story was far-fetched at best, I stammered for a moment, then managed to get a few words out.

"Yes, I read your article in *Hypothesis* and was hoping I could talk to you about your work." I think I came off sounding a bit like a fan boy.

"Who are you?" he asked, looking a little confused.

"I'm sorry," I replied. "Dr. Dunham, my name is Jack Hobbes. I'm a neighbor. I live about a mile west of here." I stuck my hand out toward him. He looked at me for a moment, sizing me up. Then, he opened the door wider and shook my hand. He stepped back.

"Okay, come in." His tone wasn't exactly decisive, and I stepped forward before he had a chance to change his mind.

The interior looked a little more like a college dorm than an old farmhouse. The living room, to the right, was furnished haphazardly and sparsely, with mismatched pieces that could easily have been gathered from dumpsters and second-hand stores. There were books and magazines scattered around on tables and chairs, and my first thought was about how studious they were. Until I noticed a couple of *People* magazines and a *Weekly World News* among them.

"What would you like to know?" Dunham asked. I stood there for a moment trying to assemble my thoughts into something resembling a coherent statement.

"Have you been able to achieve time travel?" I finally asked. Not exactly inarticulate, but reasonably lucid.

Dunham looked at me a little puzzled. I realized I was going to have to elaborate, but before I could, footsteps approached and the other scientist, Dr. Curtis, came into the room.

"What's up?" he asked. He was about the same age as Dunham, but equally unexpected. In lieu of a lab coat, he wore a white Karate-style jacket, held closed by a white belt tied around his waist. His blonde hair was shorter than Dunham's, and was neatly combed.

"This is a neighbor," Dunham replied, then he looked back at me. "Mr. Hobbes, this is Dr. Curtis."

Dr. Curtis looked at me, I thought, a little suspiciously, and he put his hand out.

"Nice to meet you," I said, shaking his hand.

"A neighbor, huh?" he said. "What can we do for you?"

I glanced at Dunham, and then back at Curtis.

"I'm sorry to bother you here at your home."

"I don't live here. I just work here."

"Oh. Well, I was hoping I could talk to you about your work."

"Are you a scientist?" he asked a little bluntly.

"No, I'm not."

"How do you know about our work?"

"I saw the article in *Hypothesis*."

"But you're not a scientist? How did you know about the article in *Hypothesis*? It's not exactly a mainstream publication."

"You're right. My father-in-law was a scientist. He showed it to me. The fact is I didn't really get much of what was said in the article. But I'm hoping I could talk to you a little about time travel."

"Did my old man send you?" he demanded.

"Uh," I stammered, confused, looking back and forth at the two of them. "I'm sorry, I don't understand."

Curtis looked me up and down, studying me for a few seconds. I glanced at Dunham again, who seemed a little uncomfortable, but I didn't know if it was for Dr. Curtis' benefit or mine.

"My father thinks my work is frivolous and a waste of money," he said, apparently trusting me enough to share that little bit of information. "He's been wanting to shut us down for a while now."

"I'm sorry, I don't even know who your father is."

He stared at me a while longer. I felt uncomfortable myself under such close scrutiny, but finally, he nodded.

"Well, I guess you don't really look like somebody who would be associated with my father." He motioned toward the living room. "Would you like to sit down?"

"Thank you so much, Dr. Curtis," I said.

"Please," Curtis said with the first smile I'd seen him accomplish, "call me O.B.Wan." The three of us walked into the living room. My face probably looked as puzzled as I felt.

"O.B.Wan?" I asked.

"O.B. Curtis," he replied. "I like O.B.Wan better than Oren Bradley."

"You can call me Sprach," Dunham said, taking his cue from Curtis.

"Sprock?" I asked. "Don't you mean Spock?"

"No, Sprach, as in *Also Sprach Zarathustra*. The music by Richard Strauss, used in *2001: A Space Odyssey*."

"Ah," I said as the pieces of the nerd puzzle fell into place. "Nice to meet you both. I've had a few unflattering nicknames in my life, but now, I just go by Jack." I realized that it was a little easier to think of these guys as O.B.Wan and Sprach than as serious scientists, at least the mental image I had of scientists.

They each sat in mismatched easy chairs. I pushed aside an Iron Man comic book and a DVD case (*X-Men: Days of Future Past*) and sat down on the saggy sofa in front of them.

"What can we do for you, Jack?" O.B.Wan asked.

"Okay," I said, realizing that I couldn't put it off any longer, "this is going to sound really strange, but back in January, I saw myself, driving my car, but with a 2018 sticker on the license plate."

"I'm not sure I understand," Sprach said. "You pictured yourself in 2018?"

"No, I didn't imagine it. I witnessed it. I was on my way to work when I saw another car just like mine. I saw it on multiple occasions, so I started documenting it." I held up the notebook. "The car was driven by me, and although I saw him several times, he never saw me. And there was no mass to it. I actually drove through it."

O.B.Wan and Sprach exchanged a look.

"What?" I asked.

99

"You said this was back in January?" O.B.Wan inquired.

"Yes, January and into February."

"Nothing more recently?" Sprach asked.

"Well," I said, feeling a little uncomfortable, "that's why I'm here. In February, I saw my future self involved in a fatal accident. I'd like to prevent that outcome if possible."

They looked at each other again, then back at me. I couldn't quite figure out the looks on their faces.

"You said you read the article in *Hypothesis*?" Sprach asked.

"Well, sort of. I really just kind of skimmed it. I'm afraid it was a little over my head."

"Alright," O.B.Wan said, "here's the thing: Sprach and I have been working for months to try to establish an Einstein-Rosen Bridge, but we've been unsuccessful."

"An Einstein-Rosen Bridge?" The term was familiar.

"A wormhole," Sprach clarified.

"Oh," I said, "Right. I've read about those in space stories. Science fiction."

"Right," O.B.Wan continued, "except that a wormhole can be opened anywhere, not just in space."

"At least, that's what we were trying to prove," Sprach said. "We just couldn't seem to do it."

"Except that you did," I countered excitedly. "It happened almost every day."

"See, I don't get that," Sprach said, scrunching up his forehead. "We kept trying to open the bridge, but we never saw anything happen."

"But I thought a wormhole was to transport quickly from one time or place to another," I said. "All I saw were images, but they didn't see me. And they could pass right through me like they were ghosts."

"As you probably know," O.B.Wan said, "opening a stable, working Einstein-Rosen Bridge requires a tremendous amount of energy." I nodded as if I *did* know. After all, Doc Brown needed

100

1.21 gigawatts to power his DeLorean time machine. "We figured that, until we got the kinks worked out, we'd start out with a low-power bridge, what I call a viewport. We didn't know what we'd be getting into, so we used a fraction of the energy in hopes that we could *see* the other side before we actually risked traversing time."

"One way," Sprach said, "view only."

"Like watching a movie," I said.

"Exactly!" they both said simultaneously.

"Okay," I said, trying to get to the part which was, to me, the most important point, "so how do we prevent my untimely death next year?"

"Have you thought about changing your route to work?" Sprach asked. His tone and facial expression indicated that he was a little surprised I hadn't thought of something so elementary and obvious.

"I did. Everything was going fine until they started doing road work on the new route. Now, I've been detoured back to the original road."

"Interesting," O.B.Wan said. "Could be explained by a number of theories."

"Really? Like what?"

"Well," he said thoughtfully, "there's the post-selected theory of time travel."

"Post-selected?" Sprach said. "That doesn't make any sense. How would that apply?"

"Effect prevents opposing cause."

"But he's not going into the past."

"It doesn't matter."

"It absolutely *does* matter!" Sprach said emphatically. "It's the basis for the whole theory!"

"What's the post-selected theory?" I asked.

They both turned and looked at me as if they were surprised I was still there.

"Oh," O.B.Wan said. "The post-selected theory holds that something that has happened can't be changed. You know the old grandfather paradox?"

"I'm not sure," I replied.

"It's a scientific puzzle," Sprach said, still sounding somewhat irritated, "an anecdote that screenwriters and movie producers have apparently felt like they've had to include in virtually every time travel film ever made."

"You go back in time and kill the person who will eventually become your grandfather," O.B.Wan continued. "Since you've done that, your father will never be born, which means that *you* will never be born. So what happens to you after you've killed him?"

"Okay," I said, "yeah, I've heard that. But I don't see how that relates to me."

"It doesn't," Sprach said.

"That by itself doesn't," O.B.Wan agreed. "But the post-selected theory basically states that events can't be changed. You try to kill your grandfather, and something happens to prevent it. The gun jams. Whatever. History is immutable."

"But it's not history," Sprach countered. "It hasn't happened yet."

"But Sprach, you're thinking only of linear time. What if time's not linear?"

"Huh?" I asked, my head swimming.

"Some scientists, including Einstein, believe that the past, present and future are happening simultaneously. That our understanding of them as three distinct states is simply an illusion. That we only see them as separate, divisible periods because of our limited perception as finite beings. So if the future really has already happened and your perception just hasn't gotten there yet, then in that sense, it's as if that accident is already a factual event and you can't change it. The road crews show up to prevent you from taking a different route to work."

"But why?" I asked. "It's not like I'm a figure of any great historical significance. Why would it be so important for this accident to happen?"

"We don't know if you are or aren't significant," Sprach said. "You're still a fairly young man. You could end up being especially important in some way."

"Or one could argue that *everyone* is significant," O.B.Wan mused. "That it's not just the people who make it into the history books who are important, but that everyone is an important part of history."

"O.B.Wan's the philosopher of this outfit," Sprach said in a feigned confidential tone.

"But if that's the case," I said, "that everybody is important, then why can't I prevent the accident that kills me?"

"Different people are important in different ways," Sprach answered. "Some people are significant simply as cogs, or as a cause leading to a greater effect. They're the pawns on the chessboard of life."

I looked at him in shock.

"You're saying that I'm disposable? That I'm just a pawn to be sacrificed for someone or something else? That I have to die so that something more important than me can happen? I'm kind of important to my wife, and to my unborn son."

O.B.Wan held up his hand in a calming gesture.

"Sprach doesn't always think about how what he says affects people." Sprach looked as if he didn't understand what he did. "It's not that your life isn't important. Admittedly, there are some people who are more historically significant than others. But, we aren't saying that this is what's happening, either."

I was feeling a little slapped around, but I tried to refocus.

"You see, Jack," O.B.Wan continued, "since nobody has been able to accomplish time travel yet, all of these are just unproven theories, anyway. At this point, for all we know, it could even be fate."

"Uh, O.B.Wan," Sprach said, "your philosopher is hanging out again."

O.B.Wan and Sprach were huddled together looking at the entries in my notebook. I had asked them exactly when I was supposed to die, based on when I witnessed the accident. They seemed a little hesitant to reveal too much, so as an act of good faith, I shared my documentation with them.

They occasionally muttered between themselves, things I couldn't hear, but I let them go for a while. They got to the last entry, where I had documented in detail what I had seen at the time that JackSimile died. After reading it, O.B.Wan looked up at me.

"Wow," he said, "that must have really freaked you out."

"Yeah, you could say that."

Sprach looked up at me then.

"JackSimile and the Phantom Fury," he said with a smile. "That would be a cool name for a band!"

"So," I said, looking mainly at O.B.Wan, "can you tell me when that final scene takes place?"

"I hate to get your hopes up," he sighed. "I'm afraid our operation has been plagued with glitches."

He closed the notebook and looked at me, and seemed to soften at my disappointed expression. In the short interval of his gaze, Sprach looked back and forth between the two of us. O.B.Wan looked down at the notebook for a second, then back up at me. Finally, he spoke.

"Okay, let's see what we can do." He stood up. "Come with me."

I stood and looked after him a little hesitantly. I wasn't sure what to expect, and it looked as if Sprach was kind of hesitant as well. I followed him as we went back out into the central hallway where I came in from the entry, but instead of going left toward the front door, we turned right. We went through a kitchen that hadn't seen an updating since the fifties. There was even an old linoleum-topped chrome table and chairs that resembled a set my grandparents had when I was a kid.

Past the old dirty gas stove, the chipped and stained farm sink, and the short, round-topped refrigerator, O.B.Wan opened a door. I could see steps leading down, and I prepared myself for a dusty, cobwebby basement that might rival an Indiana Jones set.

I saw right away, though, that I was mistaken. The stairway was modern, sturdy, and wider than most farmhouse basement stairs. When we got to the bottom, I think my mouth may have been hanging open. It looked like a movie set alright. Just not an ancient crypt.

It was fairly expansive, in length and width, as well as height. The ceiling was at least ten feet above my head, much higher than your typical old farmhouse basement. It was full of equipment that resembled heavy-duty ductwork, with metal pipes, tubes and cables all around, with a few scattered control panels. It reminded me of photos I'd seen of that Large Hadron Collider in Switzerland, though obviously on a much smaller scale.

Located in the midst of the tangle of pipes, tubes and cables was an area surrounded by a metal framework, attached to a metal chamber of some kind, roughly eight feet in diameter and about ten feet long. Inside the metal framework was a computer work station. O.B.Wan noticed me looking around.

"Yeah," he said, "I had to enlarge the basement to fit the equipment in here. The basement's much larger than the house, which is fortunate, since most of this stuff wouldn't fit down the stairs." He pointed toward the far end. "Most of the equipment was lowered in over there and assembled down here." Then, he gestured toward the other end of the lab (the term "basement" just didn't fit anymore). "Over there is HAL, our supercomputer."

"HAL?" I asked, remembering the soft, menacing voice of the computer in the movie *2001: A Space Odyssey*, and what "he" ultimately did to the whole crew of the Discovery One, except for Dave Bowman. "As I recall, he didn't work out very well for them."

"I am completely operational," Sprach said in the familiar voice, "and all my circuits are functioning perfectly." He grinned, and he almost looked as if he were proud of his accomplishment.

"Yes," O.B.Wan said with a knowing smile, "we're geeks, and proud of it."

I looked at the computer. It was screened off from the rest of the lab behind a glass wall, and consisted of several racks about six feet tall and each containing a stack of about fifteen computers. On the end of one of the racks, one of them had taped a print of the red "eye" of HAL 9000.

"It's not the biggest or the best, by any means," O.B.Wan said, "but it does the job for our little operation."

"HAL can perform up to two PFLOPS," Sprach said excitedly.

"P-FLOPS?" I repeated, feeling silly as I heard the sound come out of my mouth.

"petaFLOPS," he said in a way that I'm sure was meant to clear everything up.

"It's a measurement of computer speed," O.B.Wan said. "Up to two quadrillion floating-point operations per second."

"Okay," I said. Anything that contained the word "quadrillion" sounded like a lot, and obviously two quadrillion would be even more. But it still didn't mean a thing to me.

"Doesn't matter," O.B.Wan said, waving a hand dismissively. "It's not important to what you're wanting to find out. Anyway, this is STP." He gestured toward the tangle of pipes and cables linked by the computer work station attached to the big metal chamber in the middle.

"STP?"

"Space-Time Portal. The project I've been working on for years."

I have to admit I was astonished. Not only by the mass of equipment in this little farmhouse basement, but by the kind of work they were doing here. I had always loved science fiction books and movies, and time travel stories were always my favorite.

"How does it work?" I asked, a little awestruck.

"Well, I can show you how it's *supposed* to work," O.B.Wan said. "Come with me."

He went into the metal framework to the computer work station, and Sprach and I both followed him. Sprach swung the gate closed behind him and pulled hard to latch it in place. O.B.Wan tapped a key on the computer to wake it up, and touched an icon on the desktop.

I couldn't help noticing how similar the computer interface looked compared to my own home computer. But as the program started up, I could hear the whine of all the combined processors behind the glass wall at the end of the lab. In front of us, beyond the computer, was one end of the large chamber I had seen. It appeared to be open to the framework we were in, like the opening of a large culvert.

The desktop on the computer monitor changed to something that looked like a control panel on the bridge of the Enterprise on *Star Trek: The Next Generation*. O.B.Wan touched a button icon on the screen.

"First," he said, "this compartment we're in acts as a sort of a reverse Faraday cage. It keeps all the energy generated in here contained, and isolated from the electrical fields and other activity outside it."

I could hear a low pulsating sound surrounding us and, the compartment being pretty small, I could feel the metal framework growing warm. I also noticed a slight greenish haze developing around us, a familiar shade of green, which I recalled from each time JackSimile and the Phantom Fury disappeared.

O.B.Wan tapped some keys on the keyboard.

"Then, I enter a target, which includes latitude and longitude, along with temporal coordinates."

"Elevation, too," Sprach interjected. "If you were actually going to traverse the wormhole, you wouldn't want to appear buried in solid rock, or falling from a hundred feet off the ground."

"Yeah," I said, "I can see how that could put a damper on the trip."

Simulations showed up on the interface that resembled a topographical map surrounding a marker for the location O.B.Wan had entered, and at the bottom of the screen was a sort of scale divided into years, months, days, and even smaller increments which I assumed to be hours and minutes.

"Once I'm satisfied with the physical and temporal locations," O.B.Wan continued, "and with the duration, that's when I open the portal."

He touched a green button icon that said "Engage," and the noise coming from Hal was joined by what sounded like a muffled tenor holding a high note. O.B.Wan looked up over the monitor. The forward portion of the cage, the part connected to the big metal chamber I had seen, was glowing green, and shimmering around the edges, again, similar to my sightings of the wormhole south of my house.

"Now, if it worked," O.B.Wan said, motioning to the green glow, "that's the portal. This is where our view of the location would appear. A holographic image would display here like a 3-D movie."

"And if it was actually a traversable wormhole," Sprach added, "that's where you would enter it."

"But," O.B.Wan said with a disappointed voice, "this green glow is all we've ever seen."

"Well," I said, "it sounds like a really cool idea. If it worked."

"Yeah." O.B.Wan began shutting down the program, the tenor's voice deepened, then faded out, and the glow in front of us disappeared with a shower of green sparks. When he shut down the program, Hal quieted down, too.

"Anyway, let's see if we can pinpoint that date for you." As my ears adjusted to the relative quiet, he pulled up an activities log, a much more simple-looking program that seemed downright boring after the STP control. He opened my JackSimile notebook and flipped to the last entry, noting the date. Scrolling through several lines of data in the log, he stopped on one line.

"That's what I was afraid of," he said disappointedly. "This is one of the many entries in the activities log that just recorded gibberish."

I looked at the screen, and the entry he pointed to, consisting of a few lines of text, was indeed just meaningless groups of numbers and letters. And as he said, most of the entries on the screen were like that.

"We've been trying to figure out the problem for months," O.B.Wan said.

"I've spent hours rooting through processors and pipes and shit," Sprach corroborated. "Can't seem to find any problem."

"Sorry, Jack."

"It's an interesting idea," Nathan Rosen said, settling back in the chair in front of Albert's desk. Nathan was only thirty-six years old, yet Albert, thirty years his senior, considered him an equal and respected his intelligence. That quality was one of the things that Nathan most admired about Albert.

Nathan's forehead puckered, and he turned and looked at the blackboard again. Albert's face smiled, though his mouth couldn't be seen behind his mustache. "A number of problems persist," Nathan continued. "You would need to determine the perfect frequency to realize the stabilization. You would need a device that could generate the continuous wave and direct it at the proper locations. And you would need a tremendous amount of energy to accomplish this."

Albert nodded.

"Yes, there are a few persistent obstacles."

"But knowing you, you'll overcome them." Nathan looked genially at Albert. "You're one of the smartest people I know."

"Oh, it's not that I'm so smart," Albert said humbly, "it's just that I stay with problems longer."

"And you usually figure them out."

"Well, I sometimes have help. As I do now."

"Hold on, Albert, I don't know what I can do to help. I can't stay. I have to get back down to Chapel Hill."

"Your eyes on the equations, and your confirmation have already helped. I wasn't sure about this, and I'm still not sure how it could be done, but I have a better idea who to ask now."

"Hmm." Nathan looked at the blackboard again. "I love the elegance of your equations."

Albert's eyebrows went up and he looked at the board, then back at Nathan.

"Those chicken scratches?"

"I'm not talking about the handwriting. I'm talking about the math. There's a certain sophistication to your equations, even when you're just ruminating."

"Now, you're just flattering an old man."

"You know better than that, Albert."

Albert looked warmly at Nathan and smiled.

"Yes, I do. Thank you, my friend."

There was a light knock on the door.

"Come in." Helen slipped quietly in through the door.

"I'm sorry, but Dr. Curtis is here to see you. He doesn't have an appointment, but you know how persistent he can be."

"I do." Albert glanced at Nathan with a sigh. "Send him in."

Helen pulled the door open and beckoned Dr. Curtis into the office. After he entered, she left and closed the door behind him. Curtis smiled, but hesitated when he saw Nathan.

"I'm sorry," he said, "I didn't mean to interrupt anything."

"It's alright, my boy," Albert said as he stood up. Nathan appeared a little confused, and he stood as well. "Dr. Curtis, meet Dr. Nathan Rosen."

"Oh my God! It's an honor, sir," Curtis enthused as he stepped quickly forward with his hand out. When Nathan took it, Curtis shook it vigorously. Nathan looked curiously at Albert.

"He was that way with me the first time, too," Albert smiled.

Curtis looked from one to the other, then he focused on Albert.

"So, does this mean you might have some new information for me soon?"

"Perhaps," Albert said with a twinkle in his eye.

W hat's wrong, Jack?" Becky asked.

"Nothing," I said quickly, looking up from my plate. "Why?"

"You've just been really quiet. Quieter than usual. And you've hardly touched your dinner."

Quiet, huh? Apparently the churning in my gut wasn't as audible as I thought it was.

"Sorry, I guess I'm just not hungry."

She watched me for a second, waiting, I suppose, to see if I was going to expound on that.

"Well, that explains the fact that you're not eating. But why are you so quiet? You've hardly said anything all evening, ever since I got home."

I looked at her, weighing my options. I remembered how it went before, when I talked about JackSimile and the Phantom Fury. I didn't want to have Becky angry at me again. On the other hand, I now had proof that I hadn't just been hallucinating. More than my own documentation, I now had character witnesses.

"Okay," I said, "here's the thing: I went to see those scientists this afternoon." Her eyebrows puckered.

"What scientists?"

"The ones from that magazine your dad gave me a while back. Remember?"

The pucker went away, but I saw something else settle on Becky's face.

"Is this about seeing your future self again?"

"Well, it's not about seeing my future self *again*, because if you remember, I saw myself die. But yes, it is about that."

"I thought you got over that."

"How do you just 'get over' seeing yourself die?" She rolled her eyes, obviously sorry to see an old episode returning. "I never told you details about it, and you never asked. But I saw my future self, JackSimile, driving south, on his way to work, right down the street here – " I pointed out front, "and a gas truck blew a tire. It went out of control and rolled over, right on top of him, where it exploded.

"I got out of my car and walked around it, and I could see the truck and my car engulfed in flames. Aside from that, there was no movement. Neither one of us survived."

"Jack," Becky said with a tired-sounding tone, "that doesn't happen. People don't just see visions of how they're going to die."

"What are you talking about? There *are* people who see things like that."

"Well, okay, there are. So, what? Now you're saying you're a psychic?"

"No, I'm saying I got a glimpse of the future." I saw the look in her eyes. "I know, at first, I thought I was crazy, too. But it turns out I wasn't hallucinating. These two scientists have been experimenting with opening a wormhole into the future, and I just happened to stumble upon it."

"Jack, do you hear yourself?" Becky scoffed. "'A wormhole into the future'? You're talking about something out of a science fiction movie or a comic book."

"I know it sounds like it, but it's real, Becky. O.B.Wan and Sprach have a state-of-the-art laboratory just a mile away from here, powered by a really fast supercomputer."

"Wait," Becky said, sitting back. "'O.B.Wan and Sprach'?"

I sighed, realizing my mistake.

"Okay, I know what it sounds like. Those are just nicknames. They're a couple of geeky guys who like science fiction. But they're working in real science. A highly technical trade magazine that your dad subscribes to did an article about them."

"You know, Jack," Becky said with a tone of resignation, "it's fine. If you want to believe in fantasy, I don't care. If you want to hang out with a couple of Comic Con nerds, go for it. If you even want to go out and watch yourself drive through the future, that's fine, too. Just don't check out on me, okay?" There were tears forming in her eyes, and I knew her mood was precarious.

"Becky, of course I'm not going to check out on you. I love you. But I don't want to check out on life, either. That's why I'm pursuing this, to try to prevent my death next year."

"Fine." She sighed and gave an almost imperceptible shake of her head, picked up her fork again, and continued eating. I knew enough about the differences between male and female vocabularies to know that it wasn't really fine, but I didn't know what more to say.

We finished our dinner with a strained silence.

"One thing I don't understand," I said as we got out of O.B.Wan's car, "well, besides all the *other* things I don't understand, why did I see myself a couple of times in the past? My car was a little newer and I had 2014 tags on my license plate."

"I checked the dates of both of those entries in the computer's log," O.B.Wan replied. "One of them is just gibberish. But Sprach and I had been discouraged by our lack of success at opening a bridge into the future."

"Yeah," Sprach agreed. "We couldn't figure out why the bridge wouldn't open. So there were a few times we tried to look into the past, just to mix it up a little."

"We were just as discouraged when we didn't have any success with that, either," O.B.Wan concluded.

"And all that time, you *were* successful, you just didn't see it."

"Yeah, and I've checked the targets we entered, and there doesn't seem to be anything wrong with them. It's probably some glitch in the programming that threw everything off. It's going to take hours, if not days, to go through all the code and see where we went wrong."

"Well," I said, "maybe this will help." We were standing on the side of the road, where numerous times, I saw JackSimile and the Phantom Fury appear in a shower of green sparks.

"I don't know that it'll help us find the problem," O.B.Wan said, looking around. "Nothing short of tedious examination of the code will do that. But I still want to see where it happened, anyway."

He had taken his phone out and was busy doing something with an app.

"Okay," he said, "I have the coordinates for this end. Show me where it ended."

We piled back into the car and we went nearly a mile before I had him stop again.

"This is it," I said. "I made a note of this stand of cottonwoods flanked by the two spruce trees."

We got out, and O.B.Wan fiddled with his phone again.

"Got it," he said. He looked around, and when he spoke, his voice was a little quieter. "So, this is where you saw yourself die, huh?"

"Right back there a little ways," I said softly, remembering the terrifying scene. I took him to where the accident happened and he got those coordinates, too. But I wanted to solve the mystery. "Might it have anything to do with the earth's rotation?" I asked.

"What are you talking about?" O.B.Wan asked.

"Well," I said slowly, trying to put my thoughts into words, "you know how, because of how long it takes the earth to go

116

around the sun, a specific date is on a different day of the week from one year to the next?" O.B.Wan and Sprach both looked at me a little blankly. "Or the sun is in a slightly different location in the sky at the same time of day, from one day to the next?" I don't know if I was making myself clear or not.

"I'm not sure what that has to do with it," O.B.Wan said. He looked as if he was really trying to follow my train of thought.

"You've talked about locations in space-time," I said. "But what if, because of the earth's rotation, the coordinates you entered for a year from now are in a slightly different location?"

"Ah," Sprach said, as the confusion seemed to clear up. "No, if motion through space-time was a factor, we'd have a hell of a lot more than just a mile to account for. The earth is orbiting around the sun at about 67,000 miles an hour. Further complicating it, the sun is dragging the earth along in its gravitational field, hurtling through space at about 45,000 miles an hour in a helical pattern."

"Wait," I said, "what?" Sprach sighed.

"Okay, you probably remember simple models of the solar system which show a static sun, with all the planets orbiting around it in these neat, flat, circular paths?" I nodded, as I pictured just such a model from school. "But that's a load of bullshit. That's not the way it is at all. The universe is constantly in motion, traveling outward from the point of the Big Bang billions of years ago. Our Milky Way galaxy is not only rotating, but moving in a path through space. The sun is moving, too, and all the orbital paths of the planets around it, including earth, are following it on its journey."

He was gesturing, with the finger of his right hand representing the sun's path from left to right, and the finger of his left hand following it in a spiral pattern, representing earth's orbit around it as it moved. I could see how the movements of earth were much more complicated than that flat model led one to believe.

117

"So," Sprach continued, still moving his left finger in its demonstration, "here we are on earth, doing this weird corkscrew path through space at about twelve miles per second. If you're looking for a specific point in space, that's *not* relative to earth's location, then in a year's time, that spot's going to be nearly 400,000,000 miles behind us."

That was all it took to numb my brain and glaze my eyes over.

"Besides," O.B.Wan added, "our coordinates are simple latitude and longitude, for specific points on earth. Those don't change."

Okay, that part I could grasp. I nodded silently, still no closer to postponing my upcoming death.

"Don't worry, Jack," he added, "we'll figure it out."

With all the time we had invested lately in getting Becky moved, fixing up her house, getting it listed and sold, getting married, getting the nursery ready, coping with her pre-partum depression, well, Becky and I hadn't had an evening out for a while. So when Tim Sherman called and invited us to join him and his wife Bobbie, we jumped at it.

Tim and Bobbie were several years older than us, but we all enjoyed each other's company. They were the ones who had introduced Becky and me, and we both felt a certain debt of gratitude to them. We were sitting around a table at Carrabba's Italian Grill in Westminster, with Mike and Tanya, a couple of other friends.

"I don't get it," said Tanya with a puzzled expression on her face. "Who's Bobby Sherman?"

Bobbie looked blankly at Tanya for a moment. Then she shook her head slightly. "You know," she said, "I forget that some of my friends are ten to fifteen years younger than me. Bobby Sherman was a singer in the early seventies. A teen heart-throb with no voice. I just hated the idea of him coming to mind when my name was mentioned."

"I liked Bobby Sherman," protested Mike. "But then I liked Donny and Marie, too."

Bobbie grimaced.

"You could have kept your maiden name," offered Tanya.

"Yeah, but I didn't like that either. My maiden name was Butz, and you can imagine the grief I was given about that while I was growing up. So I decided that Sherman was the better choice of the two. Besides," she said as she turned to Tim and gave him a warm smile, "Tim is such a sweetie, I didn't mind too much taking his name."

"What about Roberta?" Mike persisted.

"He's the one that sucked," Bobbie asserted, "not me. Why should *I* change?"

"You know," Tim said, "I think I remember hearing that he's an EMT now."

"Really?" Bobbie replied. She looked at Tim silently for a moment. "Well, now I feel like a shit for trash-talking about him."

Everyone laughed a little at her mild discomfiture. Tim looked at us, apparently ready for a different topic.

"So, what have you guys been up to? We haven't seen you in a while."

"Oh, you know," I said, "just working, getting ready for the baby, so on, so forth."

"Have you picked out a name yet?" Tanya asked?

"I hear Jack has," Tim said with a smile, "but Becky doesn't care much for it."

Becky sighed and rolled her eyes, and when they stopped rolling, they were looking at me. Fortunately she smiled, so I knew her annoyance wasn't too deep.

"I'm afraid my wife just has no appreciation for fine graphic literature," I said.

"We're not naming our baby Calvin Hobbes," she asserted once again.

Everyone laughed at the name, including Becky, since she knew the issue had already been settled.

"Why don't you name him Jack Junior?" asked Mike.

"I don't know," I said, "I never cared for giving a boy the exact same name as his father."

"Jack-son?" Bobbie replied with a grin.

"What about JackSimile?" Becky suggested with a laugh. She realized too late that the name might require an explanation, since I hadn't told anyone else except her father and the nerd brigade about it. It might have passed unnoticed if not for her apologetic expression as she looked at me.

"Huh?" asked Tim. "What about JackSimile?"

"I'm sorry," Becky said under her breath, looking a little bit apprehensive. I was afraid an episode of depression might be looming.

"It's just as well," I said, leaning affectionately against her, and her dark expression seemed to clear. "You'll all know next year when I'm dead, anyway." I was trying to make it sound light-hearted, but it came off just sounding macabre.

"Back in January, I was on my way to work when I was run off the road by a car that looked suspiciously familiar. I got back on the road and almost caught up with it, close enough to see that it was my car."

"Wait," Tim interrupted, "what were *you* driving?"

"I was driving my car." Their faces looked understandably confused. "I couldn't find out any more than that, though, because the car I was chasing vanished in a shower of green sparks. It was like it drove through a shimmery green curtain into another dimension or something."

I had everybody's attention, though Tim looked as if he was expecting a punch line. Becky was looking down at the table, waiting patiently for me to finish, but likely sorry she had brought it up in the first place.

"It was the third time I saw it that I was able to get up close enough to see who was driving. It was me. I saw this several times, and each time, I made note of different details, including the year tag on the license plate: 18. I was seeing myself sometime in the next year, but each time, the car vanished in that green curtain of sparks."

"Tell them what you called it," Becky said.

"JackSimile and the Phantom Fury." That got a few laughs.

"Cool name," Mike said.

"Finally, in February, I was following my future self when I saw an FHG truck blow a tire and roll out of control, blowing up on top of JackSimile. I saw myself die."

"You should write this down," Tanya said. "That's a great story."

"Well," I continued, "it's not over yet. Becky's dad gave me a science magazine that did a cover story on a couple of young scientists who are experimenting with space-time and wormholes. They're right over by where we live. So, I met them and saw their lab, and we're trying to figure it out."

"Tell them their names," Becky suggested, smiling now.

"Dr. Oren Curtis and Dr. Joshua Dunham," I replied, knowing I wouldn't get away with leaving it at that.

"I mean tell them what you call them," Becky persisted. I shot her an annoyed look.

"O.B.Wan and Sprach," I said. "It's what they call themselves. They're just nicknames."

"Sprock?" Mike asked. "You mean Spock?"

"No, it's Sprach, as in *Also Sprach Zarathustra*. That's the fanfare that's used as the theme of *2001: A Space Odyssey*."

There was a subdued "Oh" from my audience.

"I think you're all missing the point, though," I said a little impatiently. "I'm going to die in a fiery crash sometime in the next year."

"Hold on," Becky said, "your tags expire in December. It could just as easily be December of *this* year."

I looked at her as the realization sunk in.

"Shit," I said quietly. The glimmer of a smile that formed on Becky's face brought back my annoyance at the knowledge that she still didn't believe me. But then, as she saw my expression, her face clouded again.

"Wait a minute," Tim said as he looked at my face. "You're serious about this?"

"Deadly serious."

They all seemed a little unsure about how they should respond considering, first of all, the unbelievable nature of the story, and secondly, the disparity between Becky's attitude and mine. The fact is that I knew it was unbelievable. And for that reason alone, I knew deep down that I shouldn't be annoyed at Becky, but I couldn't help it. I knew it was real.

"Why don't you take a different way to work?" Tanya asked.

"I don't know," Mike said, "remember that movie *The Butterfly Effect*? He could make some kind of change to what he saw and fuck things up even worse."

"Worse than dying?" Bobbie replied. Mike shrugged as he thought about it, but didn't say anything more.

"The fact is," I said, "I already tried that. Shortly after that, they started doing road construction on my new route, and detoured me back to my old route. They're scheduled to be done next September."

"Okay," Tim said thoughtfully, "what if you were to make other changes?"

"What do you mean?" Bobbie asked.

"Well, Mike mentioned *The Butterfly Effect*, the movie. The basic concept of the butterfly effect, though, is that small changes affect greater outcomes."

"Oh," Tanya said, "you mean like George McFly finally punching out Biff Tannen eventually made the McFlys rich and successful."

"Something like that."

I couldn't tell if they were actually getting into the spirit or just humoring me. But the idea was interesting. I had already tried to change a major – and obvious – detail. But what would happen if I tried to change some of the lesser details, things that I had already seen in the "preview"? Could it somehow affect the outcome of what I had seen? Seemed like it was worth a try. I was already going to die. Like Bobbie had said, it couldn't get worse than that.

"I'm glad you could come, my friend," Albert said, reaching for his pipe. "It's been too long."

"It has," Leo Szilard smiled, his round face lighting up. At forty-eight years old, Leo was nearly two decades younger than Albert, yet, as with his other acquaintances in the scientific community, Albert considered him an equal. "And the last time was not such a pleasant project."

In happier times, Albert and the Hungarian-born physicist and inventor had engaged in numerous discussions of scientific, philosophical, and even religious subjects. Some of the scientific discussions had even resulted in inventions, like the absorption refrigerator they had invented together twenty years earlier.

The last thing they had worked on, though, was the letter to President Roosevelt in 1939 which ultimately led to the research and development of the atomic bomb.

"Yes," Albert agreed, "the bomb did not turn out as we had anticipated."

Leo had hoped that the mere threat of the bomb would be enough to establish and maintain peace between nations. After its development, Leo drafted a petition addressed to President Truman, urging that the power of the bomb be publicly demonstrated, and that it not be used on a civilian population. He also suggested that, after the war, the bomb be put under international control to avoid an arms race between super powers. The petition was signed by Leo and seventy scientists who worked on the Manhattan Project.

The petition was never delivered to Truman, and Hiroshima and Nagasaki became the public demonstrations.

Leo had no problem speaking his mind as the bomb was being developed, and especially after it was used in Japan. He ruffled some feathers when he stated that the use of nuclear weapons was a flagrant violation of our own moral standards

"I'm hoping our committee will be a critical juncture in the bomb's misuse," Leo mused.

The Emergency Committee of Atomic Scientists, which Albert and Leo were working to form a little later in the year, would be devoted to warning the public about the dangers inherent in developing nuclear weapons.

"Yes," Albert nodded, "nuclear energy holds such promise, if used in a peaceful way.

"Like this project," Leo said, motioning to the papers they had been working on, and brightening up a little. "This was just too tempting to pass up. Thank you for inviting me to contribute."

"Your contribution was vital," Albert said. "I can't think of any way this would have worked without your unique insight and knowledge."

Leo looked with satisfaction at the papers spread haphazardly across Albert's desktop. The time had flown, but they had accomplished quite a lot. Some of the papers contained intricate mathematical equations, others were detailed working drawings.

"This should provide sufficient power for what you are hoping to accomplish."

Albert's eyes smiled and he looked at the papers, nodding in agreement.

"Yes, I feel confident that a breakthrough is within our reach."

"Well," Leo said, "I take up my post at the University of Chicago later this year, but I'll be anxiously awaiting news of the developments."

I don't know," O.B.Wan said. "There are probably as many different theories about that as there are physicists."

"It seems dangerous to me," Sprach said. "You have no idea how seemingly minor details affect the whole."

"Well, yeah," I said, "my friend mentioned the butterfly effect. But I figure that if I'm already going to die as it is, what's the harm in changing what things I can?"

"That's an extremely selfish and narrow-minded viewpoint." Sprach was getting on my nerves. "Yes, the butterfly effect can be a bitch. But it can be a bitch for others, too. Let's say you *do* change something that affects the outcome that you saw. Because that accident doesn't happen, the fire and rescue personnel are not dispatched. Since they aren't dispatched, traffic patterns along the route that they would have taken are different, and someone else is in an accident, someone who wouldn't have been adversely affected by the current scenario."

"Okay," I shot back, "but even if I'm not there, the gas truck still has a blowout, it still rolls over and it still explodes. You'd still have your deadly fiery crash and your emergency personnel dispatched."

"And you go on your merry way, fucking up the timeline in countless other ways."

Sprach tried to stretch himself up taller than he actually was. If he had been in my house, I probably would have punched him. As it was, I was in *his* house. Specifically, the living room upstairs from the lab.

"Alright, why don't we calm down," O.B.Wan said.

"Well, he's being a fucking idiot," Sprach said. "You know the kind of damage he could do, because he just wants to save himself?"

"I never took you for a religious man," I said, "But you sound like you believe in predestination or some shit like that."

"I believe in maintaining the integrity of the timeline."

"If your beloved timeline is so delicate, then what's the point of doing *anything* for our benefit?" I asked. "We try to cheat death all the time. Why wear seat belts when we're in a car? Why take any kind of safety precautions?"

"Because we don't usually know the outcome!" Sprach barked. "In this case, we do."

"You're trying to tell me that just because *you* fucked up with your programming and set your wormhole down near me instead of you, that I'm not allowed to do anything to try to save my own life?"

"Take it easy!" O.B.Wan said, stepping between us. He looked at me, his voice calm. "We're here to help."

"No, we're not," Sprach persisted, "we're here to prove that it's possible to create a man-made traversable wormhole." His voice had only slightly less of an edge to it. "All the time we're spending on his problem is time we're not working on that."

"I don't give a shit about your fucking wormhole," I growled, racking up more demerits with God. "And you can't tell me that if you were the one whose death was looming, you wouldn't be doing everything in your power to prevent it."

"Sprach," O.B.Wan said, "you're an applied physicist. You're accustomed to working on scientific problems with a practical application. This is just one more. So what's the problem?"

Sprach glared at me for a moment, then looked at O.B.Wan, squirming a little.

"We're just wasting time," he finally said, his voice sounding a little more subdued.

"We're learning. Jack documented his findings with the care and precision of a scientist. He's provided us with some valuable information, not the least of which is that our experiment was actually a success. So let's get over our differences and try to get focused on the work again."

Sprach looked at me, apparently still smoldering, but quiet. O.B.Wan turned and looked at me as well.

"Jack, personal opinions notwithstanding, I think it's safe to say that making reasonable changes in your routines and actions in an effort to save your life would be perfectly acceptable, and completely understandable."

Sprach scoffed and shook his head, but he said nothing.

"Go ahead and do what you can to prevent the outcome that you witnessed. Meanwhile, we'll get to work on tracking down the problem in our programming."

As I leafed through the notes I had taken about all my sightings of JackSimile and the Phantom Fury, it was a little disheartening to see how few of the details I would be able to change. Only two that I could find.

Concerning the first idea, several times, I had made notes about what I was wearing. Often, it was just whether I was wearing a coat or light jacket, but a few times, I could see the collar of a shirt sticking up above my outerwear.

On the morning of the accident, though, I hadn't gotten up beside him to see, because I saw the truck coming in the oncoming lane. But I was close behind him, studying details, and even though my headlights didn't illuminate him, from his dashboard light, I had gotten an impression of the back and side of a shirt collar. I had noted that there were a couple of possibilities. I went right to my closet, pulled them off the hangers and threw them away.

My other idea would require a little more time and effort. And money. I drove to a nearby car dealership. My old Fury had been with me for a long time, but maybe it was time for a change. If I didn't have the Fury, would anything else change? Maybe just the act of trading it in would trigger other things that wouldn't have happened in the previous timeline. And of course, the absence of the Fury itself would be a pretty major change.

I got some strange looks from some of the salesmen milling around in the lot. But one of them made his way toward me as I got out of my car.

"She's a classic," he said with a big salesman smile on his face. "Are you sure you want to part with her?"

"Yes, I think it's time." I didn't see the need to elaborate about the reason. He laughed as if I was making a joke.

"Lamont Washington," he said with his hand out. I shook it.

"Jack Hobbes."

"What are you looking for, Jack?"

"Something cheap but dependable," I said. "I'm afraid I can't afford much."

He nodded. If I read his face correctly, it seemed as if he might have been just a little disappointed, but it was hard to see through the salesman veneer. Anyway, having seen what I drove up in, I'm sure he couldn't have been terribly surprised.

We looked around the lot and found a couple of possibilities. One, a ten-year-old Toyota Corolla, based on miles, condition and price, was the best candidate. I took it for a quick test drive, after which Lamont and I went inside to crunch the numbers. A few minutes in, I started squirming.

"You declared bankruptcy two years ago?" Lamont said peering into his computer.

Oh, yeah.

"My ex-wife spent some time in the hospital and subsequently lost her job. Unfortunately, our insurance didn't cover very much of it."

He nodded and looked back at the computer.

"Says you also missed a couple of house payments?"

"Well, I didn't exactly miss them, but I admit I was pretty late paying them. It took me three or four months to catch up." I didn't realize that getting a new car was going to be quite *this* uncomfortable.

After several minutes of the old back and forth, and a few trips to talk to his manager, just to let me know that they were doing everything in their power to work with me, Lamont had to level with me.

"Okay, I gotta be completely honest with you, Jack, this is a little bit of a challenge. First of all, I'm afraid your car's not worth anything as a trade-in. Frankly, we'd immediately have it junked, so there's no value there for us. We've been taking in a lot of trades lately anyway, so there's just not much incentive for us there."

He took a deep breath and sighed as he continued speaking.

"Your bankruptcy and those missed house payments have hurt you, and your credit score is, well, pretty damn low. While that in itself doesn't make us unwilling to extend credit, it does make us a little more cautious. It really limits how much credit we can extend to you, especially as topped out as we are with trade-ins.

"So, here's what my boss is willing to do: If you can come up with at least a couple thousand toward this purchase, I think we have a deal."

I looked at him for a few seconds. I wracked my brain for any way I could pull that off. I was already stretched thin. I was still making sizable payments on my ex-wife, and I really didn't have any cash to spare. Why do you think I missed those payments in the first place?

"Okay," I said, "let me think about it, and see if I can round up some cash." I already knew it would be nearly impossible. After the scene I had just endured, though, I was too embarrassed to just say I couldn't do it. But I started thinking that maybe I could take some money from my savings. I didn't have a lot, but for this, maybe I could manage it.

"Alright, man," Lamont said. He stood up and shook my hand, but he didn't seem too disappointed to see me go.

That night, Becky had something of a meltdown. She had had an encounter at work with an unhappy customer. Nothing too out of the ordinary about that. In her line of work, it was common enough to come across people who just wouldn't be satisfied, but in her current state, it just made more of an impression.

She didn't purposely wake me up, but with everything that had (and hadn't) happened recently, I wasn't exactly sleeping very soundly. I heard her crying, and I found her in the nursery, pacing back and forth in the dark.

"Becky, what's wrong?" I asked, using the calmest voice I could muster.

She turned toward me, trying to stifle a sob. While it was dark in the room, dim light from the crescent moon shining through the window illuminated the rivulets of tears tracing their way down her cheeks.

"Jack, I don't know what's wrong with me."

"It's okay, honey. Dr. Janyk said that antepartum depression was fairly common."

"It's okay?" The sudden sharp edge to her voice told me that I had better tread carefully. "You don't think it's a problem that I'm feeling this way?"

"Well yes, of course, it's a problem, sweetheart," I said, walking toward her. "But it's not something that can't be dealt with. We'll call the doctor in the morning." There were large wet spots on her t-shirt, on both breasts, where her tears had been falling. The size of the spots let me know that she had been crying for a while. I took her in my arms and held her. She resisted at first, but then she relaxed and just started bawling.

I felt completely helpless, unable to do anything constructive except hold her. But eventually, she calmed down enough to be coaxed back to bed. I lay there next to her, gently caressing her arm and her shoulder, listening to her sobs finally subside. Her breathing gradually slowed and she settled into an uneasy sleep pattern.

In the morning, I called Rob, my supervisor, to let him know I wouldn't be at work. By the time Becky got up, she seemed surprised to find me still at home. Aside from that initial reaction, though, she was just listless. She seemed exhausted, as if she hadn't slept at all. But by that time, I had already managed to arrange a last-minute appointment with Dr. Janyk for the late morning.

"Mild depression?" I asked. "It didn't seem mild to me, when she was pacing and crying during the night."

"Based on what you've both described," Dr. Janyk replied, "yes, it seems fairly mild." He had longish blonde hair and spoke with a slight accent. Slavic maybe? He looked at Becky. "You've not described any desire to harm yourself. You are able to sleep, when you can relax. Your appetite does not seem to be greatly affected."

Becky nodded, apparently feeling a little better now with something to focus on.

"So, what you're saying is that it's nothing to worry about?" she asked.

"No, I'm not saying that at all. It definitely does need to be dealt with, or it could develop into a more serious depression. All aspects of your health need to be cared for, especially during pregnancy. Your health affects the health of your baby."

"You're talking about putting her on an antidepressant?" I asked.

"Well, no," he said, screwing up his face with a warning expression. "The fact is that any medication you take will cross the placenta and reach your baby. There has been research that potentially links physical issues in newborns with certain depression medication taken by the mother during pregnancy.

"That's not to say that every antidepressant will definitely harm your baby. However, there is a lot of debate concerning the potential risks. But no, for a mild depression like yours, I can recommend a support group."

"A support group?" Becky asked, her face displaying a mix of emotions.

"Yes, a group of people enduring similar conditions or situations can provide a great deal of support and encouragement to help you through the depressive episodes. Other common options are psychotherapy and light therapy. Light therapy is usually for seasonal affective disorder, which you don't seem to have. Here in Colorado, with the number of sunny days in a year, and especially during the summer time, seasonal depression is, frankly, not an issue I've encountered very often.

"And while psychotherapy may be helpful, for the level of depression that you seem to be experiencing, I'd be more inclined to try the support group first. That may be enough."

"What about work?" Becky asked, with a quick glance toward me.

"That's up to you and how you feel. Physically, you're doing well, but your job, frankly, may be a tough one for you to keep up with. Being on your feet for long periods of time can be difficult for anyone, but especially for a woman entering the third trimester of pregnancy. And the situation yesterday which seemed to be the catalyst for this latest depressive episode, well, those may come more frequently as you become less comfortable. So you should weigh your options in relation to working your job."

Options were weighed, choices were discussed, and a decision was made. Becky talked to her manager, who was aware of the situation, and began her maternity leave early. For the next few months, we would be a one income family.

My idea of taking money out of savings and trading in my car was now off the table.

"Can you begin to realize what we've done here, Albert?" Professor Wendell Curtis asked with a quiet tone of reverence, *"I think we've made history."*

Wendell Curtis was a professor of physics at Princeton University. While Albert's studies at the IAS focused primarily on theoretical physics, Wendell was more inclined toward practical application. Therefore, he seemed to Albert to be the logical person to bring this project to. Besides, he was related to young Dr. Ronald Curtis, the scientist who had been hounding Albert for the last several months. Wendell was the obvious choice.

Albert nodded, raising his eyebrows and furrowing his ample brow.

"Of course, it's only theoretical," Albert cautioned, *"but it certainly has promise."*

"More than promise. Your theories tend to be proven, Albert, if given time."

"Not all of them," Albert replied humbly. *"I have to admit I'm still a little embarrassed by the 'cosmological constant' incident."*

"Psh!" Curtis dismissed with a wave of his hand. *"That was almost twenty years ago. And the cosmological constant was only a portion of the theory."*

"Yes, but it was a rather important portion. The universe is not static as I stated. I didn't believe what my own equations were telling me and I disregarded them."

"Well, that just proves my point! Even though you drew a wrong conclusion, your theory was still correct."

Albert smiled and looked down with an almost bashful expression.

"So," he said, getting the conversation off of himself, "you believe this is workable?"

"More than workable, I think it's going to be a turning point in human history." Albert raised his eyebrows again, giving his face an astonished look. "Oh, yes," Wendell continued, "man has dreamed of this for generations. We've just proven it's possible."

"Theoretically," Albert said again.

"Theoretically," Wendell conceded. He placed his hand on the stack of papers on the desk in front of him. "But Albert, all of this work is phenomenal!"

"Well, you helped a great deal," Albert said. "And even with the part that I brought, I can't take full credit. There was a lot of input from a number of great minds."

"I understand that, and I'll make sure that Kurt and Leo and Nathan – and you, of course – all get ample recognition."

"Good. So, what are your intentions?"

Wendell looked at the stack of documents for a moment. His face gradually spread into a large smile.

"I want to build it. I want to try it out!"

Albert smiled in return.

"Yes, I thought you might. With your drive, I knew you were the one to see this through."

Wendell was almost salivating as he contemplated what lay before him. Science books would be rewritten. His name would become famous.

"My family will shit themselves by the time this is over." For the third time, Albert raised his eyebrows in response. "Sorry," Wendell said. "They've just never thought much about what I do."

"Oh," Albert said. "I didn't realize that."

"Yes, if anything, they could be the ones to disprove your Theory of Relativity. My relatives are anything but *gravitational. They tend to push me away every chance they get."*

Wendell smiled about his joke, but Albert frowned.

"I'm very sorry, my friend."

"Oh, don't be," Wendell said with a wave of his hand. "I've gotten used to it by now."

"That doesn't include Ronald, does it?"

"Who?"

"Dr. Ronald Curtis, your cousin."

"I don't have a cousin. Ronald or otherwise."

I got a taste of driving a different car to work on some mornings, if Becky knew she didn't have to go anywhere that day. I admit I felt a little safer driving her car on those days, even though I knew I wasn't yet in the time period in which the accident would happen.

Becky started attending meetings with the support group that Dr. Janyk had recommended. She was hesitant at first, but after a couple of meetings, she started to feel a certain camaraderie with the other women in the group. It didn't take long for her to feel as if it could actually help.

In early November, I came home from work and was looking through the mail that had been delivered that day. I was leafing through the stack when I came across a simple white postcard. It was the registration renewal card for the Fury.

I held it as if it was stuck to my hand. I felt a feeling of horror, almost revulsion, looking at it, but I couldn't let go. I considered my options. There were really only two. Pay the fee and get the tags, or don't pay it and let my tags expire. If I let it go and got caught driving on expired tags, I would have to pay a hefty fine, along with the fee for renewing the tags anyway. If I paid the fee and put the new tags on my car, the Fury would be all set for the fiery date with destiny I had envisioned.

But I also knew that *not* getting the tags was no guarantee that the accident would be prevented. Either way, I was in completely uncharted waters. And I was still no closer to knowing when the scene in question was destined to occur. Over the last couple of months, the nerd herd had scoured all the coding in their programming and had failed to find any anomalies.

For now, at least, I decided to postpone renewing the tags.

I started leaving for work earlier and driving slowly. I was becoming a timid old man of a driver. Whenever I saw headlights coming toward me, I would slow down even more and move as far to the right as I could. Fortunately, at that hour of the day, it wasn't often that I encountered oncoming traffic.

Some days, though, I would feel weird, like a premonition or something, and I would call in sick. I'm not proud of what I was becoming, but I didn't want to die.

Rob was, as usual, understanding. At first.

But apparently I didn't realize how often I was doing it.

"Jack, is there anything wrong?" he asked one morning after I got to work.

"What do you mean?"

"Seems like you've been sick a lot lately." I had called in sick the day before.

"I'm sorry," I said. Considering that I had told Becky and her father, and four of our friends about JackSimile and the Phantom Fury, I quickly debated with myself about whether or not to reveal my fears to Rob. "Lately, Becky's been feeling pretty bad and, taking care of her, I just haven't been getting much sleep myself." Apparently I wasn't ready.

"That's too bad," he replied with his typical understanding demeanor. "I'm just concerned, though, because HR has noticed." He glanced down at the paper in his hand. It looked like an official company memo. "I'm afraid I've been instructed to issue a verbal warning."

I wasn't sure how to respond. I had always tried to be an ideal employee, and had never received any discipline of any kind. More than anything, I just felt embarrassed. I looked at Rob for a few moments, searching for a reply.

"Okay," I finally said, perhaps one of the least meaningful responses I could have given.

"I'm sorry Becky's been feeling so bad," Rob said, looking equally embarrassed. He really wasn't the kind of person you usually find in management. "And I'm sorry you haven't been feeling well, either. But you really need to try to get to work more regularly."

"I understand," I replied, anxious to move on and immerse myself in my work. Rob patted me on the shoulder and smiled, then he left.

He was back a few hours later.

"Jack," he said in a panic, "where's the shipment for Boulder Walmart?"

"It's on the truck. Why?"

He thrust a couple of sheets of paper at me and took off for the loading dock. I looked at the papers. I recognized them at once. I had just packed up the orders a little while before. A big one for the Boulder Walmart, and a much smaller order for a local 7-Eleven.

Except that I had them switched. The 7-Eleven would have been buried under the huge order being sent to them, and the order now about to leave for Walmart would have barely filled a shelf. The routines I had developed for myself helped me to work quickly and accurately. Because of that, I was the best employee they had in the shipping department. This wasn't like me.

I looked up as Rob came back, breathless.

"He hadn't left yet," he said. "Jack, this is going to require a written warning. I'm sorry. This could have cost us a lot of time and money, not to mention damage to our relationship with these accounts."

I nodded. I understood. It was a stupid mistake, one easily remedied now that Rob had stopped the delivery, but it could have been a disaster for the two customers had the shipments gone out. And for us.

Having received a verbal warning and a written one all in one day, I was now suspicious of everything I did. I slowed down so that I could minutely examine everything before it went out. I managed to get through the rest of the day without threatening to topple any other businesses, but I didn't get nearly as much done as I was accustomed to.

Needless to say, I was glad when I could finally leave.

I don't know why it didn't occur to me before! All this time, I've been trying to think of ways that I could avoid being in the middle of the coming accident. Why not try to prevent the accident from happening in the first place?

I was walking toward my car after leaving work. What a shitty day it had been! (Sorry about the language, God, but it was.) But with those two separate warnings in my head, and the tension and terror that was ultimately the cause of them, I saw a gas truck drive by up on I-70 as it sped past over the parking lot. The truck had the Farm and Home Gas logo on the tank. And it was as if something clicked in my head.

I quickly got in my car and, putting my lunch bag aside, I got out my phone. I found two locations for FHG. One was downtown, and I assumed it was the corporate office. The other was a couple of miles away, north of where I was, but still in this industrial part of town. That's where the truck would have come from.

Or *will be* coming from.

I started up my car and started driving, going over in my head how to approach it. My first thought was to pose as some kind of official in the industry. But knowing nothing about the gas industry, I knew I wouldn't be able to pull that off.

I really couldn't think of any option that didn't make me sound like a nutcase. Maybe I should be accustomed to that by now, but I guess you never get used to being thought of as crazy. Unless you really are crazy and don't even think about it.

I guess that could offer a little comfort.

It didn't take me long to get there. I could see the tangle of pipes and smokestacks before I even arrived at the gate. As I pulled up to the main entrance, I still didn't know what I was going to say.

I shut off my car and just sat there looking at the door, my breathing rough and jagged. A truck drove between me and the building, breaking my stare, and my eyes followed the truck. It was just like the one I had seen in the fateful preview.

I took a deep breath and got out of my car, walking with steps that were a little wobbly. I pulled open the door and walked in to the building. A woman looked up at me. She had been looking at some papers spread out in front of her on the dirty counter. She smiled at me.

"Hi there," she said in a voice that was a little louder than was necessary in the little front office. "What can I do for you?"

Judging by the roadmap of wrinkles across her face, she seemed to be belatedly blonde. She also apparently thought that she was thinner than she was. The buttons on her denim shirt were straining against their buttonholes, and as I approached the counter, her impressive muffin top made me wonder how she had fastened her jeans. I noticed the FHG logo emblazoned across the breast pocket. Quickly averting my gaze up to her eyes lest she think I was staring at her breasts, I cleared my throat.

"Good afternoon," I squeaked. I cleared my throat again, a little more forcefully this time. "My name is Jack Hobbes." I paused, much longer than I had planned. The lady behind the counter decided to fill the pause.

"Hello, Mr. Hobbes. I'm Mary."

"Nice to meet you."

She nodded and smiled, though her eyes looked puzzled. Well, this wasn't awkward at all! I decided that, whatever I was going to do, I better get on with it.

"Mary, I wonder if I could trouble you for some information. I'm curious about how often and how extensively your trucks are serviced."

She squinted at me, no doubt trying to figure out what the hell I was up to.

"I'm sorry?" she asked, shaking her head.

"Okay, here's the thing. I'm a psychic, and I saw a vision of one of your trucks involved in an accident. The front tire blew out early in the morning a few miles northeast of here. The truck rolled onto a car and it exploded, killing both drivers. So I'm just hoping to be able to prevent this tragedy from happening."

I know, as it was coming out, it sounded pretty damn dumb to me too. But I figured that psychics are taken seriously at least slightly more than someone who claims to have seen the future as a time traveler.

But Mary? I couldn't quite gauge her reaction. She was watching me closely and listening intently, but so far, her face seemed blank.

"You know, Mr. Hobbes," she finally said, "I'm fascinated by that kind of stuff. So tell me, what's it like when you see one of your visions?"

"Uh, well, it's scary," I said, playing along. "It's like I'm right there."

"Wow!" She smiled a kind of awe-filled smile. "That must be amazing!"

"It is," I replied a little impatiently. "So, Mary, about your truck maintenance?"

"Yeah, each vehicle is maintained regularly. So you really don't have anything to worry about. If there's anything wrong with any of them, our mechanics will find it and fix it."

"Okay, but the thing is I saw it. It's going to happen."

"Well, if you saw it and it's going to happen, then who's to say we can do anything to prevent it anyway?"

I hesitated, since she had expressed the very thing that I had been encountering. Everything I've attempted lately, to try to change the outcome of my "premonition," had all met with failure.

My hesitation seemed to have registered with Mary.

"You know," she said, "things happen for a reason. We can't change something if it's God's will."

"If it's God's will, then why would he just taunt us with a glimpse of what's coming if he's not going to give us a chance to do anything about it?" My religious past came rushing back. "In the Bible, all the warnings he gave to foreign nations and kings were with the option of them repenting and saving themselves, of changing the outcome of the warning."

"Okay, but like I said, our vehicles are well-maintained. If there's a problem, it'll be taken care of."

That's probably the best I could expect. I sounded the warning. I probably should have left it at that. But I wanted to be absolutely sure the warning was heeded.

"Any chance I could talk to your maintenance people?" I asked.

"Mr. Hobbes, they're a busy bunch of folks."

"I understand that, but I just feel it's imperative that they understand the dire situation. One of your trucks is going to blow up. One of your drivers is going to die."

I didn't mean for my voice to sound as hard as it did. The look on Mary's face told me my comment wasn't taken in the spirit in which it was given.

"I think it's time for you to leave," she said. "I don't want to hear any more of your threats."

"I'm sorry, Mary, I didn't mean for it to sound like a threat. I'm just trying to prevent a tragedy."

She looked at me for a couple of seconds.

"Okay, when does this accident happen?" she asked.

"I don't know," I admitted. "I don't know what the date is. I just know it's sometime within the next year, and a little after five o'clock in the morning."

"Which truck?"

"I'm afraid I don't know that, either."

"Who's the driver who gets killed?"

"I don't know."

"You know, I hate to say it, Mr. Hobbes, but you're kind of a sucky psychic."

"I know. Believe me, I wish I could conjure up more details, more useful information."

"Well, I'll pass along the information you've given me and thank you for your time."

I nodded, knowing that was likely as far as it was going to go. As I turned to leave, I could see that the early look of fascination on her face had been replaced by a "what a loon!" expression.

I muttered "thanks" and "goodbye" and walked out the door. I squinted into the sunshine, unimpressed by its false hope and deceptive cheerfulness. I opened my car door and slid in behind the wheel.

Mary's questioning at the end of our conversation had stirred something in me. "Which truck?" she had asked. Good question! If only I had noted specifics about the truck when I was witnessing the accident. I had seen the blowout of the front left tire. I had noticed how the truck temporarily went off the pavement, then overcompensated when steering back up onto it, which then caused it to roll.

But I had not noticed details about the truck itself. License plate, truck number, physical blemishes. All the numerous times I had seen the Phantom Fury, I had noted all kinds of details like that. But I had only seen the gas truck one time, and only for a few seconds before the wreck.

After it crashed into JackSimile and the Phantom Fury, I was so focused on trying to see any sign of life through the smoke and flames that I didn't take note of seemingly superficial details.

Those superficial details sure would come in handy now!

After my unscheduled stop, I got home later than usual. Becky picked up on the kind of day it had been the moment she saw my face. She was sitting on the sofa, throw pillows propped up behind her, but she still looked uncomfortable.

"What happened?" she asked.

I shook my head and sighed.

"Just a shitty day." I went and sat down beside her. I didn't want to burden her with my problems, but she seemed interested, and her mood seemed pretty good, so I decided to elaborate. "I got a couple of warnings at work today. One about the time I've missed, and one about a screw-up with a couple of orders."

"I'm sorry, Jack," Becky said sympathetically. "I know how you've always taken pride in your work. That must have been a blow."

"Yeah, but it's over now. Well, until tomorrow, anyway." I smiled ruefully at her. "How are you feeling?"

I was holding one of her hands. Her other hand was resting on her belly, and I wasn't sure if it was because of discomfort or just because of the convenience of its proximity. With my free hand, I reached over and caressed her belly. At seven months, it felt pretty taut.

"I'm fine," she said with a sigh. I looked at her as if I didn't believe her. "Well, you know, I'm always uncomfortable lately. But aside from that, I'm doing fine. I met with my group today, and that helped."

"That's good," I said, and I let go of her hand and put my arm around her, careful to keep from dislodging the pillows. Becky leaned into me and tilted her head against my shoulder.

"I know you believe you're going to die sometime soon," she said, changing the direction of the conversation, "and I know you're worried about that. But honey, please don't let that take you over. You're a safe driver. You're doing everything you can to survive every day."

"Yeah, but what I saw isn't dependent on just me. It's the truck that causes the accident. I don't have any influence over other drivers or vehicles."

"None of us do. Ever. We just do the best we can and hope we get through it. We can't let worry infect the rest of our lives." She turned her head and looked up at me. "You know all your routines I made fun of a while back? I miss those."

"What are you talking about?" I replied. "I still eat Honey Nut Cheerios on Fridays."

She shook her head, but she smiled. It was good to see. It hadn't been around much lately.

"Your routines were comforting to you. But lately, you've been so busy trying to change the future, you've abandoned those old routines. And you're more stressed out than ever."

"I'm just trying to maximize the time I have with you, and little Calvin."

"You mean little William."

"Whatever."

A white haze of smoke swirled languidly around Albert's head as he puffed thoughtfully on his pipe. Sitting alone at his desk in his office at the Institute for Advanced Study, the excitement of the previous weeks of discovery and invention was now tempered by a feeling of apprehension.

He sat back in his chair and sighed, looking around his office. The chalkboard still displayed some of the work that had gone into the latest project that he had just finished and given to Professor Wendell Curtis. It was good work. Albert was proud of what he and his friends had accomplished in such a short time.

But had they been manipulated in some way? Who was this Dr. Ronald Curtis, who claimed to be related to Wendell? Over the course of several months, he had shown up repeatedly, often at the most inopportune times.

But now, Albert wanted to speak to him. His love of fair play made him want to give Curtis the benefit of the doubt, the opportunity to explain himself. However, when he had asked Helen, she said she had no information on how to contact him.

Albert thought about all the conversations they had had over the last several months. To the best of his recollection, they had all centered around Albert's work. He could not remember any personal information about Curtis, other than his spurious claim to be Wendell's cousin.

It was troubling, and Albert didn't know why. It's not as if he had been working for some kind of unscrupulous entity. Curtis had not hired him, or even influenced his work in any specific way. He had encouraged Albert, even pushed him at times. The work that resulted from that pressure, and from Albert's collaboration with his friends in the scientific community, was good. Better than good, it was outstanding. Wendell had called it a turning point in human history.

But Wendell had also said he had no cousin.

His pipe now spent, Albert put it down on his desk. He sighed as he stood up. Perhaps a walk outside would clear his head. It was late summer of 1946, and the weather was beautiful. Maybe that would provide the distraction that he needed, to focus on his current work.

He walked out of his office, muttered to Helen that he was going for a walk, and went out into the bright and warm summer day. He realized it was the noon hour when he saw several faculty members enjoying the sunshine, eating their lunch in the courtyard area behind Fuld Hall.

Albert wanted to be alone with his thoughts, so he turned toward the woods, beyond the courtyard. He didn't get very far.

"Hey, Dr. Einstein." He turned and saw young Dr. Curtis approaching him. "How are you, sir?"

"I'm fine, young man. How are you?"

"Fine, thanks."

"I think, perhaps, a more pertinent question, though, might be, Who are you?"

"Huh?" Curtis frowned in confusion.

"I was speaking with your cousin yesterday, Professor Wendell Curtis, at Princeton University."

"Oh, yeah?"

"He informed me that he doesn't have a cousin. He doesn't seem to know who you are."

"Well, we haven't seen each other in a while," Curtis replied. He smiled, but Albert thought he noted a flash of nervousness. "He probably just doesn't remember me."

"Professor Curtis' memory has never seemed deficient."

"Dr. Einstein, what are you trying to say?"

"I'm giving you the opportunity to defend your claim and your identity. I'm sorry to say that you haven't convinced me."

"I'm sorry, sir," Curtis said. "I don't really know what to say. I am who I am." Albert looked at him with an expression of disappointment. "But I thought you said you didn't have any contact with Professor Curtis."

"I hadn't for a year or two. But he is the one I took my research to yesterday."

"Your research?" Curtis replied with mounting excitement. "You mean the project we've been talking about for the last several months? You finished it?"

"I did."

"What did you discover?"

"Young man, I will not be talking to you about my project any further until you can tell me exactly who you are and what you are after."

"What I'm after? I just want to know about your work. I'm fascinated by it."

"I'm sorry," Albert said, turning from him. "Please don't contact me anymore."

"Doctor Einstein, wait!" Curtis said, grabbing his arm. Albert pivoted unsteadily, nearly falling, as Curtis pulled him back.

"What do you think you're doing?" somebody shouted. Curtis turned toward the voice. Albert looked in that direction and saw a few of his colleagues approaching them.

"Nothing," Curtis said. "I'm just having a conversation with Dr. Einstein."

"Not like that, you're not," said Dr. Rivers, a young biologist that Albert had greeted once or twice.

"Look, just back off. I didn't mean to grab him, but I don't mean him any harm." Curtis' voice cracked as it took on an edge of fear.

"Then let go of him."

Curtis looked at his hand and seemed surprised that he was still holding on to Albert's arm. He let go.

"There, I let go, okay?" Curtis said. "So just leave us alone."

"Dr. Einstein?" Dr. Rivers said. To Curtis' consternation, he wasn't backing off.

"I'm fine, thank you," Albert said. "I just want Dr. Curtis to leave."

"You heard him," Dr. Rivers said defiantly to Curtis.

"Dr. Einstein, please," Curtis pleaded. "I just want to talk." But without even thinking, he reached out toward Albert again. Before he could grab his arm, Rivers was on him, pulling him away from Albert.

Curtis struggled and another faculty member came to Rivers' assistance. They each grasped an arm and pulled Curtis away from Albert. Curtis tried to fight them off and, seeing his chance with Albert slipping away, he tried to swing his arms free. He managed to shake Rivers loose, striking him in the cheek with his elbow.

As Curtis turned toward his other opponent, Rivers came to his assistance, punching Curtis in the eye. Curtis was taken by surprise, and ended up on the grass.

With Albert's colleagues standing over Curtis, Albert quietly thanked them as he made his way back into the building. He wasn't necessarily afraid of Curtis. He was more afraid of the uncertainty and suspicion that had now formed around him.

He was confident that his friends would make sure that Curtis left the grounds now. Albert would make sure that Helen, and others on the faculty, know not to let him back in.

In mid-December, the new tags arrived in the mail. I had put off renewing them, but as the deadline approached, I decided that it would be better to have them on hand. Now that they arrived, I put them aside. If I put the new year tag on my license plate on New Year's Day, I would still be covered. And hopefully, I'll live through December.

Becky was feeling better emotionally. The group really did help. In the beginning, she had met with them a couple of times a week. After her mood started to stabilize, she had reduced it to once a week. Dr. Janyk had indicated that it would likely only take a few weeks to experience beneficial results. Now, with Christmas approaching, despite the physical discomfort Becky often felt, she was in a joyous mood and was considering dropping the group altogether.

My mood, though, kept getting darker. How could I just happily accept that at some time in the next few months, I was going to die a violent, fiery death? That I was going to be snatched away from my beloved wife and child, leaving Becky a widow and little Calvin half an orphan?

Not even Becky's profusion of beautiful and ornate Victorian-era Christmas decorations could keep the darkness away for long.

"When we met, I told you that my father thinks my work is frivolous." O.B. Wan paused and pondered the steam sinuating up from his espresso on our little table at Starbucks. "I'm afraid it's actually more serious than that."

I frowned, wondering where he was going with this.

"My father has long considered me a hack, a failure. He was always so driven."

"Well, you must have been, too," I said, "to get to where you are now." He shrugged.

"As far as he's concerned, I've never grown out of the comic book nerd stage. He considers me the family embarrassment." He sighed, still watching the steam. "I had hoped that the article in *Hypothesis* might have given me some credibility with him."

"I'm sorry," I said quietly. He shook his head a little and glanced up at me. I still wasn't entirely sure why he had asked me to meet him here. I guess he just wanted someone to listen.

"The reason I'm telling you this is that my father is trying to shut me down."

"What? How can he do that? And why?"

"How is easy. Cast aspersions on me. Denigrate my work. The fact that I haven't published any successful results makes that a simple matter for him. So, to others, he can make me look like the silly childish comic book nerd that *he* still sees me as.

"As for why, that's a more involved subject. Part of it is that he thinks I'm wasting family money pursuing this. Which I'm not. The money was in a trust fund for me. My father doesn't have access to it anyway. Well, unless he manages to get me declared incompetent."

"Can he do that?" I asked in a tone of disbelief.

"I don't know. Money talks, as they say. And he's got plenty of it, himself."

"Then why would he be so hot to get his hands on yours?" I asked. He sighed and shook his head again.

"To a lot of people who have money, there's never enough."

"Well, you said the money was *part* of it. What else?"

"Competition, jealousy, resentment. And knowing my father, that's probably the more likely culprit."

"Your father's jealous of you?"

"Of my work."

"Why? I'm afraid I don't understand."

"My father has been focused for most of his life on trying to generate a traversable wormhole. He's shown some promise a few times, but never could accomplish it.

"And now, here I come, just a few years into my career and I get closer than he ever did, along with receiving recognition and adulation."

"I would think he'd be happy for you, and proud."

"Yeah, I've heard that from others, too. But I guess my family is not your typical family. There's always been competition, the desire to one-up everyone else. It's been like that for at least a couple of generations. My father was always at odds with his father, too, so I guess I'm nothing special. From what I've heard, Grandpa was kind of a black sheep, as well."

"Wow," I said. "I guess by comparison, I had a lovingly boring upbringing."

He looked at me with a sort of wry smile.

"I envy that," O.B.Wan said. "I wouldn't know what a normal family looks like." He took a sip of his espresso, then set the cup back down. "Anyway, I didn't want it to come as too much of a shock to you, just in case he succeeds in shutting me down."

I felt a chill slither down my spine as I realized that I had one more thing working against me in my quest to not die.

"How much of a chance do you think there is of that?" I asked.

"I don't know," he replied quietly. "Maybe none. But with my old man, you never know. He can be ruthless."

"What about Sprach? He can vouch for you."

"Yeah, but you may have noticed that he's something of a comic book nerd just like me."

"Hmm, maybe more," I said.

"As far as my father's concerned, Sprach is as much of an embarrassment as I am. His endorsement wouldn't mean a thing to him."

I shook my head and sighed as I looked at O.B.Wan over my cup. I took a sip, then set it down.

"Well, all things considered, I think you turned out pretty well." He smiled a little, the first positive smile I had seen from him. "And if you ever need a character witness of any kind, I'd be happy to help."

"Thank you, Jack. I want you to know I really do appreciate that. And if there's anything I can do for you, just let me know."

"Well, there is one thing."

"Name it."

"Don't let me die next year."

I stood at the little table by the front door, where we always placed the mail. I was contemplating, for the two hundred and thirty-eighth time, the white envelope from the Department of Motor Vehicles. Peeking out through the little cellophane window was a sticker with the number "18."

It was Christmas Eve, and I had just over a week before I had to put the sticker on my license plate.

"Jack!" Becky called. Her voice sounded strained.

I put the envelope back where it had been languishing and went to the family room, where Becky was on the sofa. She was breathing heavily and her face was agitated.

"What is it, honey?" I asked, suddenly tense, but eager to transfer my anxiety from myself to Becky.

"I think I'm in labor," she said, struggling to pull herself up. I rushed to her side and helped her.

"Are you sure? It's too early." The baby wasn't due till next month.

"No, I'm not sure," she replied with an irritated tone. "But I'm having contractions."

"How far apart?"

"I don't know. I'm not wearing my watch." Her irritation was growing with each question I asked. "I need to call Dr. Janyk."

I pulled my phone from my pocket and found his private number.

"Do you want me to talk to him?" I asked.

She tersely shook her head no and held her hand out. I pressed the little green telephone receiver button and handed the phone to her as it rang.

Becky looked incredibly uncomfortable as she waited, but she seemed to relax just a bit when I heard Dr. Janyk answer. She managed to hold her irritation in check as she explained her symptoms to him.

Neither of us had planned on a Christmas baby, although I know that people born near a holiday, especially Christmas, often feel cheated giftwise. But while I wasn't averse to the idea, I knew we didn't want the complications that could come from the baby being a month premature. So I waited anxiously, listening to Becky's responses to the doctor's questions.

She silently motioned to me, tilting her free hand toward her mouth, asking for a drink. I rushed to the kitchen and got her a glass of water. By the time I got back to the family room, she was lying down on her left side, facing the back of the sofa, and doing some deep, rhythmic breathing.

As I stood there, she took the glass from me and nodded her thanks. She lifted her head a bit to take a sip, and I took the glass from her again.

"Okay," she said in the phone, "yes, and it's feeling better already."

I placed the glass on the end table, and I knelt down beside her and started rubbing her back, which I knew often ached. Becky finished up with Dr. Janyk, then handed the phone back to me, careful to not move too much so I could keep working on her back.

"Braxton Hicks," she said quietly.

"Ah," I replied. False labor, or Braxton Hicks contractions. We had heard about them early in the pregnancy, but apparently both of us had forgotten about it when they appeared.

She stayed on her left side, doing her rhythmic breathing, and I kept kneading her lower back until she rolled over to face me. When she did, her face had changed. Her expression was no longer tense and upset.

"Thank you," she said.

"Of course. You're my sweetie." I said it as if I was uttering a simple statement of pure logic.

Becky smiled. She lifted her head and pulled the pillow out from under it, and she took my hand. I got up from the floor and sat down on the sofa where the pillow had been, with her head on my lap.

"I'm sorry I was so irritable with you a few minutes ago," she said.

I looked down at her and shook my head.

"Don't worry about it. You've got a pretty good excuse."

"You're a good husband," she smiled. I leaned down and kissed her forehead. "You're going to be a good father, too."

"I hope so." I thought about O.B.Wan. While I couldn't imagine the level of father and son animosity that he described, I knew father and son relationships often had a tendency to flare up into a not so fun dynamic. I hoped that my boy and I could work through those times quickly and effectively.

Then, I realized that those episodes usually came in the son's teen years.

Long after I'll be gone.

We spent a quiet Christmas day together, relaxing, exchanging a couple of presents. It was very low-key, and it was one of the most pleasant Christmases I've ever had. Later in the day, we packed up some food to take to Becky's father, and we had dinner with him.

A few times, I caught myself savoring moments – flavors of food, favorite Christmas songs, the sound of Becky's voice and laughter, the tilt of her head, and the soft skin of the back of her neck. Things that I loved, but I realized that they now caused a pang of sadness.

As if it was the last time I would be able to enjoy it.

"Son of a bitch!" O.B.Wan said quietly. He was sitting at the STP control computer in the lab, studying endless lines of what looked to me like gibberish, while I sat nearby reviewing, again, all the notations I had made in my notebook. It was the last week of December, and I was feeling desperate.

"What is it?" I asked. He stared at the screen a little longer, then he turned toward me.

"Well, I seem to have found the problem," he said. Before he could continue, we heard footsteps coming down the stairs. We both looked toward the door as it opened and Sprach came in.

"What happened to you?" I asked when I saw his face. His right eye was surrounded by purplish-grey. He put his hand up to his face, as if he had forgotten about it.

"Oh, I was hanging a picture," he said dismissively. "I slipped and fell off the chair." He looked at both of us. O.B.Wan's gaze seemed a little more intense than mine. "What's up?" Sprach asked.

"I was just killing time," O.B.Wan said, "and I figured I'd have another look at the code. I decided to start with the sections that you examined, you know, get a fresh set of eyes on it." He looked back at the screen. "I couldn't believe how quickly I found the problem, which you, somehow, didn't see." He looked back up at Sprach, who suddenly seemed a little nervous.

"Really?" Sprach said. "You found out what's wrong?" The excitement he was trying to inject into the statement didn't sound quite convincing. "What happened? Did I misplace a decimal or something?"

"Yeah, I found it. It's not a misplaced decimal, though. Two lines of code inserted here that has nothing to do with my original program. Directions to override my place and time markers." O.B.Wan's face was hard. "This wasn't a mistake. This was a deliberate act of sabotage."

"'Override your place and time markers'?" I asked. "What does that mean?"

"I gave directions for the wormhole to display traffic on I-25. I wanted someplace busy, to make sure it was working. It never did, so I thought that the experiment was not successful. Then, you come along and tell me that it *did* work, but that it was showing up over a mile away, and early in the morning. And nothing was showing on the portal. Odd, since I was always setting it for later in the day, when there would be more activity to witness.

"So, now I find these deliberate commands to override those original directions. My experiments weren't unsuccessful. They were tampered with."

"Who would do that?" Sprach asked weakly. O.B.Wan made a face.

"Don't insult me with that innocent act. There are only two people who have had access to my program. And there's only one person who could have tampered with the system without my knowledge."

"I don't understand," I said. "If it's so obvious, why didn't you see it before?" O.B.Wan turned to me.

"The program that drives STP is extremely complex. There are hundreds of thousands of lines of code. When we were checking it before, we split it up. Sprach and I took different portions of it, but this part is in a section that he took each time. I

160

don't know, yet, if there are other bits of spurious code in the parts he took for himself, but you can bet I'm going to go through the rest of it very carefully."

"Come on, man," Sprach said with a somewhat pleading tone. "Why would I do that?"

"You tell me," O.B.Wan said, standing now, and turning to face Sprach. "Did my father get to you?" Sprach's nervousness seemed to be increasing as he looked back and forth at us. "Is that it? Did he offer to supplement your pay if you'd sabotage my system, keep my work from succeeding?"

Sprach was nervously shifting his weight from one foot to the other, but he didn't have a response.

"Get the hell out of here."

"O.B.Wan, come on, man," Sprach said, as the pleading tone turned almost into a whine.

"You can call me Dr. Curtis," O.B.Wan said. "I don't want to see you again."

In the years following Albert's big, collaborative project, he devoted much of his time to warning the public about the dangers of nuclear proliferation. He also worked to promote civil rights for black people, and for Zionist causes.

Upon the death of Israel's first president, Chaim Weizmann, in 1952, Prime Minister David Ben-Gurion offered Albert the position, through Israel's ambassador in Washington. While the office of president was primarily ceremonial, it was explained that it "embodies the deepest respect which the Jewish people can repose in any of its sons." Albert appreciated the great honor bestowed upon him, and while he was deeply moved by the offer, he declined.

In April of 1955, Albert was taken to Princeton Hospital with internal bleeding from a ruptured abdominal aortic aneurysm. He died the next day. He was 76 years old.

"I can't imagine a world without Albert Einstein." Professor Wendell Curtis stared out the window of his office at Princeton University. It was a vacant stare, not really focused on anything. Hearing a murmured agreement, he turned around to face Kurt Gödel.

"Yes," Kurt said. "I miss him already."

"You and Albert were very close, weren't you?" Wendell sat heavily down at his desk.

"Yes, we were. We enjoyed many discussions walking home together from the Institute."

"What kinds of things did you discuss?"

"Oh, various things. God, physics, Adele's cooking." Both men smiled sad smiles. "You must have been close to him, too."

"Not as close as I would have liked," Wendell admitted, staring blankly at his desktop. "I had lost contact with him for a while. But we renewed our friendship nine years ago when he kindly included me in our collaborative project. We maintained contact from time to time after that. I owe Albert an immense debt of gratitude."

"How so?"

Wendell looked up at Kurt and took a deep breath, slowly letting it out.

"I had just been experiencing an inertia that I couldn't seem to get past. A lack of motivation. My wife, after a long bout with mental depression, had committed suicide. Our young son, Jeffrey, was there. He was six years old. Apparently she had killed herself in the morning. Jeffrey was there with her dead body all day long until I got home."

"How horrible," Kurt said, frowning and shaking his head in an expression of sympathy.

"I was distraught, but the weeks after that were even worse, if that's possible. Before that, I had immersed myself in my work, which may have contributed to Marcia's depression, because I was never around. I was detached from Jeffrey. I didn't know what to do with a six-year-old boy."

"What did you do?"

"My sister and her husband had wanted children, but couldn't have any. She offered to take care of Jeffrey while I was at work, and, even though my family can be a contentious lot, I gladly accepted her offer.

"But as for my work, well, I had done some important work before that. But some of it had been appropriated by the military. I had a hard time with that, seeing work I had done with the aim of bettering life being used, instead, to take life.

164

"Albert's dropping that project in my lap was exactly what I needed to renew my enthusiasm."

"So? Have you made it?" Kurt asked quietly, leaning forward. His voice betrayed a subtly excited undertone.

"I'm an applied physicist," Wendell replied with a half-smile, his first mirthful smile that day. "I'm driven to turn the theoretical into reality. It took me a while, especially since I was working on it outside the university. I used my connections when it was necessary, but I did the work on my own."

"And?"

"And it's amazing!" he grinned. "There's so much potential! The good that can be done with this is limitless!"

"If you don't mind my asking," Kurt said meekly, "how do you know it won't be misused like your other projects?"

"Well, I don't," Wendell confessed, and a flicker of fear darted across his face. "Especially with that impostor claiming to be my cousin back then. And now, the fear of Communists has swept over everyone. But I'll be taking steps."

Kurt smiled and nodded appreciatively.

"And how is Jeffrey?" he asked. Wendell sighed.

"I should have done so much more with him, Kurt. He's a very angry boy. He hates me." He raised his eyebrows in an expression of exasperation. "But then, don't all fifteen-year-old boys hate their fathers?

"I'm afraid I'm out, sir," Dr. Joshua Dunham said to Professor Jeffrey Curtis. "He found those commands I planted. He kicked me out."

"No" Curtis said, banging his fist on his desk. "It's too soon! We haven't found what we need, yet."

Curtis was a big, aggressive man. Despite being seventy-six years old, he was still an intimidating person with a blustery voice and a big, fleshy face that tended to flush when he was angry. *Accustomed to getting what he wanted, this was one of those times.*

They were sitting in Curtis' office at his home. Curtis had held a teaching position at the University of Colorado in Denver. He had retired nearly twenty years ago, though, and felt as if he had no legacy. Others in his family had done important, meaningful work. But all he had was tenure. He wanted more.

"I'm sorry, sir. I did everything I could." *Dunham was contrite. Having just lost his main job, he was hoping that he didn't lose his supplemental one in the same day.*

Curtis thought for a bit.

"We'll have to sneak you back in there somehow. You have to go back again."

"I can't! Albert won't speak to me. You see what happened last time," *and Dunham touched the bruising around his eye.*

"Don't be such a pussy! Why didn't you fight back?"

"I did *fight back. But it was two against one. Besides, that's not the point. Albert doesn't trust me. He knows I'm not related to your father."*

Curtis sighed disgustedly. He looked at Dunham for a few seconds through narrowed eyes.

"Wait, Einstein's not the one to talk to anymore, anyway," *he said.* "You said that Einstein passed the research over to my father. He's *the one you need to see."*

"Sir," *Dunham said, his voice cracking with emotion,* "with all due respect, it won't work. Your father knows, too. He's the one who told Albert that he doesn't have a cousin."

"I can't believe you were so fucking stupid. I never told you to say you were his cousin. I said 'a relative.' Something vague, ambiguous."

"I'm sorry, sir."

"And you still haven't found out what it is that makes Oren's equipment special?"

166

"No, sir. Apparently, I don't – didn't have access to everything there. I guess I never fully gained his trust. I don't know why it works with his equipment but not with yours."

Curtis kept his eyes trained on Dunham. Dunham cowered under his red glare.

Finally, Curtis shook his head and sighed again.

"Well, I guess it's going to require more persuasive methods."

I finally put the new tags on my license plate on New Year's Day. I felt like a prisoner taking that long walk to the gallows. I just didn't know quite how far away it was.

I managed to make it through the first couple of weeks of January without wetting myself, and I actually did my job without damaging any of our clients. As before, I took longer to do my work, so I could make sure I hadn't missed anything or confused orders.

When I was at work, I consciously focused on the job I had to do, and at times, I could even make it through a one to two hour stretch without obsessing about dying. That doesn't mean I didn't think about it. I wasn't apathetic about my death by any means. But I was numb in a way, caused, I think, by an absolute lack of any idea of what to do.

The first couple of days in January, I took a different route to work. The route I had initially tried was still closed due to construction. But I took a long way, heading north first – the exact opposite direction from my job – then gradually working my way back around by various country roads. The first day, I was nearly a half hour late to work. So, on the second day, I left a half hour earlier. I was only ten minutes late that day. Rob was getting pissed.

I mentioned to Becky the possibility of my getting up at three o'clock in the morning, to facilitate the new route, but her look was enough to make me dismiss the idea. I kept taking my usual route, but more slowly.

There were times when, on that one mile stretch of road just south of my house, I caught myself looking in my mirror, for no apparent reason. Eventually, I realized that I was watching for my past self. I understood that, very possibly, *I* was now JackSimile, and that I was being scrutinized by my past self. But I always remembered belatedly that JackSimile didn't see me. It was a one way view. So I would draw my attention back to the road in front of me, and continue on my way in my Phantom Fury.

But I still felt safer on the days when I drove Becky's car.

Imagine my delight when her transmission went out.

I sighed as I hung up the phone. I had been talking to Rube, our auto mechanic. I turned to Becky who was standing nearby, her hands unconsciously clasped as a support under her belly. Besides looking incredibly uncomfortable, she was also wearing a look of apprehension.

"So, what's the damage?" she asked.

"They can rebuild it for about $1800."

She rolled her eyes and gave her own sigh.

"I'm sorry, Jack."

"It's okay, honey. It's not your fault. It just reached the end of its time." That simple statement caused an involuntary shudder as I realized I could just as easily be talking about myself.

"How long?"

"He said it could be done in a couple of days, barring any unforeseen complications. But since it's Friday, they won't be able to start on it till Monday. So, best case scenario, we'll have it back Tuesday evening."

Her eyes started filling with tears, and I couldn't help it. I went to her and held her. She put her arms around me and the tears came.

"Sweetheart," I said soothingly, "it's alright. Really. It's just four days."

"And $1800."

"Oh well, it's only money." I thought that a light-hearted response might help.

"It's only money we don't have," she replied, looking up at me. So, I was wrong.

"Don't worry. We'll manage. I can take what we need out of savings." She put her head back against my chest and snuggled up to me.

"And you're not mad about that?"

"Of course not. I mean, obviously, I'd rather use all of our riches for something fun. Like retirement or college tuition. But car maintenance is a necessary thing."

"How did I ever get so lucky?" she muttered.

"I think *I'm* the lucky one."

"Yeah, you're so lucky, married to a fat blob."

Still holding her, I leaned back so I could see her, and the motion cause Becky to look up at me.

"I'm married to the most beautiful woman I know," I said, using a loving but firm tone. I could already see her expression soften. "I'm married to the mother of my little son, Calvin – "

"William," she interrupted with almost a smile.

"– and the woman I want to spend the rest of my life with."

Still teary-eyed, she scrutinized me for a few seconds. I started feeling a little self-conscious under her gaze, so I broke her stare and leaned down to kiss her. And yes, with her crying, her kiss was a little slobbery.

I didn't care.

"Jack! Jack!" It seemed as if the voice was coming from a distance. "Jack, it's time!"

"What? I didn't hear the alarm."

"No alarm, Jack," Becky said. "It's Sunday. But it's time." Her voice had an urgent tone to it. It took a couple of seconds, but her meaning cut through my consciousness like scissors through an umbilical cord.

I was suddenly awake, and I looked at Becky. It was dark, but there was enough light to see that she was propped up next to me, breathing heavily and rhythmically.

"How do you feel?" I asked breathlessly.

"Okay at the moment," she said between breaths, "but it's about to start again." She had barely finished speaking when the next contraction started. She tensed up, but started her faster panting, focusing her attention on the rhythm of her breathing.

I raced to the closet and grabbed a shirt and pulled on my jeans. Becky's stuff was in a bag that we kept by the front door, so I was the only one who had to get ready. I sat on the edge of the bed and hastily pulled on some socks and slipped into some shoes, as Becky's breathing slowed. The contraction was over.

I stood up and ran around the foot of the bed, slipping on the wood floor. I grabbed the post of the footboard on my way past, to steady myself and to slingshot myself around to Becky's side.

"It's okay, Jack," she said with a tired smile. "We'll make it. There's time."

How could she be so calm? Didn't she realize that we were about to become parents?

I helped Becky up, treating her as if she was a delicate tea cup or something. She was walking deliberately, and with her feet kind of far apart.

"How long?" I asked.

"A few minutes," she said as she slipped her feet into some shoes. "The last one came after about seven minutes."

I helped her down the stairs and into her coat, then I pulled my jacket on.

"Oh!" I exclaimed, "what about Dr. Janyk?"

"I called him, just before I woke you." She held up her cell phone. "He's expecting us."

I nodded and grabbed her bag. Then, with my other arm around her back, I helped her out the door, instinctively pulling it hard behind me. (No, I still hadn't fixed it. I've been a little distracted.) We went down the front steps, I pulled open the passenger door and helped her in.

I tossed Becky's bag into the back and jumped into the driver's seat. The old Fury roared to life. Okay, it wasn't really much of a roar, but it started, and I shifted into gear, slinging gravel behind us as I sped out of the circular driveway.

I headed down our county road when my phone rang. It was early for a phone call, especially on a Sunday, but I thought it was probably Dr. Janyk. I answered it without looking, keeping my eyes on the road. It was O.B.Wan.

"Hey, O.B.Wan," I said, "I'm a little busy at the moment."

"This is important," he said. He sounded out of breath. "Could you come to the lab."

"Not right now. Maybe tomorrow."

Suddenly, I noticed headlights, and above them, I saw the FHG logo. With a sinking feeling, I looked over at Becky. She had slipped down in her seat, panting through the next contraction. Her head wouldn't have been visible above the top of the seat.

In that horrible instant, I realized that, nearly a year ago, I had not only witnessed my own death, but also the death of my beloved wife and child. I just hadn't seen her.

"Oh my God," I said.

"What?" O.B.Wan said. "What is it?"

"The gas truck."

I was doing nearly sixty miles an hour. I knew I couldn't coax much more than that out of the Fury, to sail past the truck before it crashed. And even if I could, I didn't know if that would allow me to avoid the accident, or if it would just cause me to plow into the truck sooner.

I hit the brakes at about the same time I saw the puff near the truck's front tire. I was aware of Becky exhaling sharply as her seat belt tightened around her.

My awareness seemed to be heightened as, in slow motion, I watched the little truck waver and tip slightly. It went off the side of the road a little ways, and I saw the wheels turn back toward the road. Just like I knew it would, the truck bounced back up onto the pavement, but at too sharp an angle. I could even see the driver turn the wheels back, trying to turn into the skid, but it was too late. At the speed it was moving, the only thing it could do was tilt over.

The truck's momentum had tipped it up onto its right wheels, and it seemed to hang there for a moment, still sliding, before it finally crashed over. The rounded tank on the back of the truck offered little resistance, and the truck rolled once. It bounced a little on its tires before tipping for a second time.

The slow motion agony of seeing all this play out in real life was more than I could take. I felt a tear slip down my cheek as I thought about Becky dying in mere moments. Our story was about to end, stopped abruptly before we reached our happily ever after. And our baby's story was going to end before it even began.

The truck rolled a second time onto its back and exploded, filling my ears with the deafening concussion, and in that moment, I realized that I really had hit the brakes sooner than in the "preview." In my premonition, the truck didn't explode until it was on top of the Fury. But I also knew that it wasn't enough to change the outcome. We were skidding relentlessly toward the conflagration, the tires screeching on the pavement, as I felt the heat and a shock wave from the explosion.

I was aware of Becky, just coming out of the contraction, and pushing herself up to see over the dash, wondering where all the noise and light were coming from.

Suddenly, there was a shower of green sparks around us, and the truck, engulfed in the orange and blue flames and the cloud of black smoke, was gone.

It just disappeared.

A moment later, I realized that *we* were the ones who had disappeared, because we reappeared in a field. The Fury was still moving, my foot was still on the brake, but there was room ahead of us. And in the dirt, the tires dug in and we jerked to a stop. I heard Becky utter another little gasp at the last jolt of the seat belt.

Still in shock about whatever had just happened, I looked first at Becky.

"Are you okay?" I asked.

She nodded slowly as she looked out the windows, trying to peer into the darkness.

"What just happened?" she asked quietly.

"I'm not sure," I replied just as quietly, coming down from my adrenaline high, "but we seem to have narrowly avoided an unpleasant end."

A light came on to my left, and I looked over my shoulder. I saw the back of a white clapboard farmhouse, and I recognized that we were parked behind the ChronoLog laboratory. The back door opened and O.B.Wan came running out.

I opened my door and got out as he approached the car.

"Are you alright?" he asked excitedly.

"Yes," I replied a little shakily. "You did this?"

He nodded like a giddy little boy.

"Yes, I created a traversable wormhole!" He almost squealed. Before he could explain further, though, I heard Becky gasp behind me. Turning back around, I could see her tensing for another contraction. It couldn't have been more than two minutes.

"Okay, let's get you both inside," O.B.Wan said, suddenly all business.

"We were rushing to get to the hospital," I said as I ran around to the other side of the car. I opened Becky's door and knelt beside her as O.B.Wan followed me around. I was holding her hand, waiting for it to relax. When it did and her breathing slowed, I looked up at O.B.Wan. "I don't think there's going to be time now."

"No, probably not," he said. "Let's go."

I helped Becky out of the car and closed the door. I quickly introduced her to O.B.Wan as we walked toward the back porch. O.B.Wan led us into the house through the kitchen, through the central hallway, and into the living room. I hurried to help Becky get comfortable on the sofa, gathering pillows from around the room and tucking them against the arm. I helped her get her coat off and turned her on the sofa, helping her lean back against the pillows and get her feet up. Just moments after she settled back, the next contraction started.

She grasped my hand as she breathed through the contraction, focusing on my face. It seemed to me as if the contraction lasted forever. I can't even imagine what it was like for her. But eventually, she relaxed again.

A few minutes later, I saw O.B.Wan hovering nearby.

"Have you ever delivered a baby before?" I asked him. He shook his head and looked nervously at his watch. I looked back at Becky and got my phone. Dr. Janyk was expecting us at the hospital, but that wasn't going to happen.

Suddenly, the loud, industrial-strength buzzer attached to the doorbell sounded, making me jump and drop my phone. O.B.Wan rushed to answer the door.

Thinking it was particularly early for visitors, I found my phone again. I was getting ready to call Dr. Janyk when O.B.Wan rushed back into the room, leading someone else. He was a man of average height, average build and average looks. In fact, I had a fleeting thought that if I ever had to describe him to anyone, I wouldn't know where to start.

There was one noteworthy thing about him, though. He was carrying one of those doctor's bags like you used to see in movies, once upon a time when doctors used to make house calls.

"Sorry it took me so long," he said. "There were emergency vehicles all over the place just west of here."

"Did you stop?" I asked, suddenly feeling a little guilty, and sorry for the driver and his family.

"I asked if they needed any help," he replied with a puzzled expression, "but they said they had it under control. No survivors, unfortunately."

I sighed helplessly toward O.B.Wan, as the doctor was shrugging out of his coat. The doctor acknowledged me with a nod, but he turned his full attention to Becky.

"Hi there," he said in a cheerful tone, "I'm Dr. Collins."

"I'm Becky," Becky replied wearily.

"Nice to meet you, Becky. So, tell me where we are. How have your contractions been going?"

"They're about a minute long, and they *were* five to seven minutes apart. But we had kind of a rough ride over here," she looked pointedly at me, "and the last one came after maybe two minutes."

"Okay, and how are *you* feeling?"

"Pretty tired, and my mouth is dry." O.B.Wan abruptly turned and left, but within a minute or so, he was back behind the sofa holding out a glass of water to Becky. He was also holding a stack of towels which he placed on the back of the sofa. Becky smiled and thanked him quietly.

"Well," Dr. Collins said, "why don't we have a look?"

He took the top towel and slipped it under Becky's backside. He pushed her flannel nightgown up over her knees, and helped her slip her underwear off, and I noticed that O.B.Wan made an abrupt about face. Sitting at Becky's feet on the sofa, Dr. Collins did a quick examination.

"Well, you're not fully dilated yet, but you're close. Shouldn't be too long."

During one of the spaces between contractions, I called Dr. Janyk and let him know the situation. He was extremely cautionary at first, but he sounded relieved when I told him that a doctor was present.

Even with the doctor there, though, O.B.Wan still seemed to be nervous. He had left the living room to the three of us, but out in the hallway, he kept pacing back and forth and looking at his watch.

Now that Becky had settled down, and was no longer having to hike around, being jerked against the seat belt and hurtling through wormholes, her labor seemed to adjust, too. A half hour after we got there, the contractions were still two to three minutes apart.

Dr. Collins left the sofa to Becky and me until he was actually needed, so I sat where he had been, at her feet. I held her hand, acting as her focal point when she was in the midst of a contraction. Between contractions, though, our conversation took quite a different turn.

"Jack, that truck blew up right in front of us!" she said quietly. I just nodded in response. "I heard the explosion! I felt the heat! I saw the flames!" I nodded again. "Then, we were here, and that truck was nowhere around." I raised an eyebrow, waiting for her conclusion. "So, does this mean that wormhole stuff was real?"

Again, I nodded. Never one to gloat or say 'I told you so,' I was happy to let the facts do it for me.

"Honey," she said, "I'm so sorry I didn't believe you."

"Well, let that be a lesson to you, young lady. I know what I'm talking about." Okay, I agree, that resembled 'I told you so.' But I was only joking, too. Sort of.

Fortunately, my joke wasn't too subtle that Becky couldn't get it because, even in her current state, her lips curved up into a little smile.

The next contraction started and she squeezed my hands. Looking intently into my eyes, she kept up the quick, rhythmic breathing technique. I knew it was getting pretty bad. Beads of sweat were standing out on her forehead, and the pain was showing on her face.

It was at the end of this contraction that I heard a bang from out in the hallway as the front door was flung open. It was followed by angry voices and footsteps on the wood floor.

We were both startled, and we turned toward the hallway. Poor Becky was feeling pretty worn out but, still curious, she peered up and over the back of the sofa, which was toward the hallway.

The first person I saw was a large man with thin, white hair. He was surprised to see us there, and he stopped at the arched entrance to the living room, looking at us with a puzzled expression.

Then, immediately behind him, Sprach appeared. Stopping abruptly before he ran into the old man, he also seemed particularly surprised.

"What the fuck are you doing here?" he said to me. "You're supposed to be dead."

"I said get out of here, both of you!" O.B.Wan said, catching up with them. "This is private property."

"Son," the old man said, turning his attention back to O.B.Wan, "you're not in any position to throw us out."

"What the hell are you talking about, Jeff?"

"How many times have I told you to call me Dad?"

"You may be my father, but you've certainly never been a dad. This is my place! I want you both out!"

"I don't care what you want," his father snarled. "There's something I need from you."

179

"You're not getting anything from me," O.B.Wan said, and I was impressed by his firm resolve.

The old man, still somewhat distracted by our presence, seemed to want to deal with us first.

"Who are you?" he asked. It wasn't an inquiry, it was a demand for information. Dr. Collins was the first to speak up.

"I'm Dr. Peter Collins. I'm here to deliver a baby," and he gestured toward Becky. "Who are you, sir?"

The old man seemed surprised again, this time about the idea of a woman giving birth in this house. He was clearly disappointed to find people other than O.B.Wan here, and he paused to look at Becky, ignoring Dr. Collins' question.

"He's the one I told you about," Sprach said, pointing at me. "Saw himself die and wanted to fuck with the timeline."

"I don't give a shit about that," the old man said menacingly. "I just don't want them here."

"You heard him, asshole," Sprach said to me, ramping up his antagonism to a level he hadn't attempted before. "All of you get the fuck out of here."

"Back off, little man," I said, stepping between him and Becky, and surprising myself a little with my own bravado. He attempted to pull himself up to his fullest height, and was still coming up a little short.

I heard Becky gasp and begin breathing quickly behind me, and I knew that the next contraction had started. I turned toward her, and Sprach, taking advantage of my distraction, grabbed me by my left sleeve and yanked me in the direction of the door. He did so in such a way, though, that my right arm had pretty good momentum as I turned. I punched him in the face, satisfied that both of his eyes would match, now.

Turning my back on him where he fell, I went back around the sofa to help Becky. Dr. Collins had taken my old position at her feet, and was discretely examining her.

"She's close," he said quietly to me. "What's going on here?"

"I don't know," I replied under my breath. "I know there's bad blood between them, but I don't know what his father's after."

While focusing on Becky, and her hand squeezing mine, I also tried to hear what was going on between O.B.Wan and his father. Sprach had picked himself up off the floor and had taken refuge in Curtis' shadow, but he was still hurling daggers at me with his eyes.

"I need to know how your system works, Oren," Curtis said.

"It doesn't. Didn't your little spy tell you?"

"Josh is the one who sabotaged it. I know you know that, and I'm sure that, by now, you've fixed it. So I'm asking you again, tell me how it works."

"You do know that wasn't a question, right?" O.B.Wan asked, a little smug in his smartassedness.

"How the fuck does it work?" Curtis yelled, and I noticed Becky jerk a little, startled.

"Get out of my house," O.B.Wan said quietly but firmly. Becky began to relax, her rhythmic shallow panting changing to a slower, deeper breathing, as O.B.Wan pushed the two of them toward the front door.

"Go help him," she said quietly.

"Are you sure?" I asked, blotting the sweat from her face.

She nodded, trying, I think, not to show how exhausted and uncomfortable she was.

"He saved our lives. Now, he can use our help. It's two against one."

"Go ahead," Dr. Collins said. "I'll look after Becky."

I nodded back at them. Becky's hand was still in mine. I kissed it, then stood up. Shafts of light stabbed through the window from the rising sun, and I knew we had been here for almost two hours. So far, it had turned out a little differently from the way I had envisioned our baby's birth.

I got to the front door, just as O.B.Wan opened it to push his unwanted visitors out, only to find a couple of bruisers waiting there on the porch. Curtis smiled, and I realized then why he had so easily allowed himself to be pushed. He knew he had backup waiting there. O.B.Wan didn't seem terribly surprised, though.

Curtis and Sprach started walking back into the hallway, followed by the goon squad, and O.B.Wan and I backed up.

"You can't do this," O.B.Wan said. Curtis smiled again.

"All you have to do is show me your secret and I'll be out of your hair."

"Forget it."

"This isn't going to end well for you." I was chilled by Curtis' tone. I had issues with my dad when he was alive, but they were nothing compared to this.

"What are you going to do? Rough me up?"

"If that's what it takes, son. Or worse. Do you really want to put your friends here in harm's way, just so you can hold on to your secret?"

"You're threatening all of us? I always knew you were a bully, but I never realized how far it went."

Curtis scoffed.

"It's weird. They say that boys eventually become like their fathers. You actually sound like *my* father."

"I wish I could have known him." It wasn't a sentimental statement. It was more reminiscent of a little boy's angrily saying "I wish *he* was my father."

"Yeah, that's too bad." No sentimentality there, either. "You're just like him. He was a fucking holier-than-thou bleeding heart do-gooder who wouldn't share his biggest discovery. Just like you."

"What do you know about his biggest discovery?"

"I know he had focused his attention on wormholes for many years. I know he was excited about some discovery. I know he

182

talked about it with others using glowing terms. He even said he thought that it would be a turning point in human history.

"He was a friend of Albert Einstein, and they collaborated on the project with some other giants of the time. And apparently they had been successful.

"I tried to follow in his footsteps, to build on what I had learned from him, which wasn't much. The bastard refused to share his knowledge. Or maybe it was just with *me* that he refused to share."

Curtis' voice became more bitter and cold the longer he talked about his father.

"I'm curious how you know what he talked about with others, if he wasn't sharing with you," O.B.Wan said.

"It doesn't matter how I know."

At the same moment he was saying that, Sprach was blustering.

"Because I was there, asshole," he said.

"Shut up," Curtis hissed.

"I thought so," O.B.Wan said, sounding totally unsurprised. "It seemed like the morning logs had been completely wiped some days, when there should have been at least some automatic start-up and monitor activity. Come to think of it, you also knew that Jack should have been dead this morning. So you knew when it was supposed to happen. The program didn't scramble the activities log. You did."

Sprach smiled a cocky smile that I really wanted to punch off of his face.

"So, you snuck in and used my STP system to go back and interact with scientific 'giants of the time,' and you're not happy about that?"

Sprach seemed smug, but Curtis growled, taking the conversation back.

"I need to know how. That technology should have been mine. Being able to do it on *your* equipment doesn't help me at all."

"And helping you has always been the most important thing."

"I've always had to help myself. My old man never would. Even when I was six years old and my mother killed herself, he couldn't be bothered with me. He passed me off to his sister. The fucker was never around."

"Sounds familiar. I'm surprised you want anything to do with him. Why do you even care about his technology?"

"'A turning point in human history'? It's huge! But he never told me about it. He never published anything about it. He didn't bequeath it to me. Very little money, either, for that matter. The selfish son of a bitch took his pet project, this life-changing technology, to the grave."

"Did you put him there?" O.B.Wan asked. I looked sharply at him, wondering what I had gotten myself into.

"I never said that," Curtis said in a voice lacking any tone or emotion. Or surprise at the suggestion.

"I noticed you didn't deny it, either. I know it was some kind of accident in his office at home."

"You know what they say," Curtis shrugged, "more accidents occur in the home than anywhere else." He left a meaningful pause here. "And I'm sure you'll want to avoid an accident here." He cast a quick glance at his backup, who pulled pistols out of their coat pockets. "Fact is, I'd prefer to avoid it, too. So I suggest you start talking."

"You really think multiple gunshots are going to look like an accident?"

I was kind of wishing O.B.Wan would quit goading him. I had already narrowly escaped dying once this morning. I wasn't interested in just changing the cause and location.

"I don't really care what it looks like," Curtis said. "I just need you to tell me about the guts of your technology." He flicked his head at one of his goons with guns, who stepped forward and pointed his pistol at O.B.Wan's forehead.

"Why won't you just admit you killed your father?" O.B.Wan persisted. I had to give him credit. Even in the face of potential filicide, he bravely pressed on.

"Why are you so fucking fixated on that? It was over thirty years ago."

"You just seem so blasé about the whole idea. You're such a tough guy, I'd think you'd want to take credit for ridding the world of an asshole."

"Would that make you feel better?" Curtis asked, getting more impatient and agitated, and making me more nervous. "Is that what it will take to finally make you shut up about it? Fine, I killed him. Now, can we get on with this?"

"Absolutely," O.B.Wan said.

Just as I was feeling surprised by his sudden change of heart, I heard multiple footsteps coming up the stairs at the back of the house. The basement door opened and several men dressed in black tactical outfits, including Kevlar vests, swarmed in from the kitchen with rifles drawn.

After the cocky attitude that Curtis and Sprach had displayed just a few minutes before, it was a pleasure to see the surprise on their faces as the cops leveled their weapons at them. Curtis' two gorillas dropped their pistols and put their hands up. Curtis looked annoyed. Sprach looked downright afraid.

I admit it was a joy to see.

The cops quickly picked up the discarded weapons, then, putting the goon squad, Curtis and Sprach against the wall, they were all frisked and handcuffed.

"Dr. Jeffrey Curtis," one of the men said, "I'm Deputy Scott Hopper, Weld County Sheriff's Department. You're under arrest for murder, unlawful entry to commit a felony, attempted robbery, and threat of bodily harm. For now."

The two goons were arrested for all but the murder. Sprach was charged with unlawful entry and collusion to commit a felony. Deputy Hopper then read them their rights, just like on TV.

I heard a high-pitched squeal from around the corner in the living room, forcibly reminding me that Becky was in labor.

"Can I go to my wife?" I asked Deputy Hopper. He was busy directing his men to take their prisoners outside, and he just nodded curtly at me.

I ran a few steps to the arched entry and into the living room. Dr. Collins was hunched over on the sofa, while Becky, her hands gripping the underside of each of her thighs, was straining as hard as I've ever seen anybody strain.

I squatted down beside her and, as she stopped straining long enough to take a breath, I lightly touched her shoulder. She was barely able to acknowledge it, though, as she immediately started pushing again.

From that point on, I had no awareness of what was happening out in the hallway or in front of the house. All my attention was on Becky, and I found myself straining with her, feeling for her, blotting her sweat, giving her water when she needed it.

Professor Wendell Curtis sighed as he looked out the picture window of his home in Littleton, Colorado. Ten years after picking up and moving away from Princeton, New Jersey, with his sixteen year old son, Jeffrey, he was more alone than ever.

It was 1966, and Jeffrey, now twenty-six years old, had never let up in his hatred of his father. If anything, his hatred had only grown after they moved away.

Infected by his antagonistic family, Jeffrey saw Wendell as the cause of all his unhappiness. Wendell had to agree, to an extent. Following that horrific day when Jeffrey was six years old, when his mother committed suicide in front of him and lay dead all day long while the boy cried, Wendell essentially gave his son to his sister, Elizabeth. He had experienced clashes and animosity from her throughout his life, and when she offered, he wanted to believe it was signaling a change in their relationship.

She took care of Jeffrey while Wendell was at work at Princeton University. Wendell didn't know how to relate to a little boy, so she was the one who actually raised him.

Jeffrey's dreams and night terrors, usually involving his mother's dead body, was more than Wendell, in his own grief, felt able to handle. Elizabeth became Jeffrey's 'mother' and savior, and his greatest influence.

By the time Wendell realized the magnitude of the damage she had done, the boy was approaching his teens, and he realized that it was probably too late. Still, though, he decided to do something, to try to salvage his relationship with Jeffrey.

He took Jeffrey back from Elizabeth, to both her and Jeffrey's resentment. The transition was anything but pleasant, and he spent more hours in arguments and screaming matches with his son than he cared to remember. He tried to get Jeffrey to see a psychiatrist, but the boy wouldn't consider it.

To his credit, Wendell cut back his hours at the university so that he could spend more time with Jeffrey. To his dismay, it resulted in little more than more time to fight. In time, Wendell made a difficult decision. He left his position at Princeton and moved himself and Jeffrey to Colorado, hoping that getting away from his family, particularly Elizabeth, and getting into a more idyllic setting, might help to calm Jeffrey and ease their relationship.

The country setting a few miles southwest of Denver, with views of the Rocky Mountains, did wonders for Wendell's nerves, when Jeffrey was at school. When Jeffrey was at home, it was worse than ever. Added to all the reasons his son hated him was now the fact that he had taken Jeffrey away from friends and family.

The one point about Jeffrey that Wendell took comfort in was the fact that he still did very well in school. Despite his many and assorted problems, he was such a smart boy. Eventually, he proved just how smart by majoring in applied physics, and by graduating at the top of his class.

"Just like his old man," Wendell thought. But, of course, it wasn't at all like him.

Wendell proudly attended his graduation, only to be snubbed by Jeffrey. By that time, of course, Jeffrey had moved out on his own and had virtually nothing to do with Wendell.

Wendell took comfort in something else. In fact, in his later years, he pretty much obsessed about it. Having brought the result of The Project with him, he used it frequently, especially now that Jeffrey was gone.

To actually be able to see the past or future was something that he had only dreamed of. With what he had been able to build, he could only witness various points in time, not actually interact with them. But still, the thrill of actually seeing a historical event that he had, before, only read about gave him chills.

Perhaps, someday, he would put the time, effort and money into building a larger version of his prototype. He was certain that, with enough power, he could actually cross over into those other times. But for now, he was happy witnessing well-known historical occurrences, preview unimaginable future events, from the safety of his home.

A turning point for him was when he got the idea to look at his own future. He wondered what the future held for himself and his son, if they would ever reconcile.

What he learned, though, was far from comforting.

Dear Oren,

By the time you read this, you will be twenty-one years old, and I will have been dead for several years. I am truly sorry that you will never know me. But this seems, to me, to be the best solution to my dilemma.

I know about your love of physics, and I know that you will, eventually, be a passionate advocate for many different disciplines in the world of science. I also know of the obstacles which you face in your pursuit of your passion.

Because of that, I hope that this will ease your difficulties, to some degree, at least.

This letter is accompanying documents concerning a trust fund that I have created for you. The bulk of my estate, I am leaving to you anonymously. The funds will, I hope, help you to advance your dream of being a brilliant physicist.

The other portion of your inheritance is my true legacy. Not only mine, but that of several other intelligent scientists, caring humanitarians and good friends.

The Project, as we called it, was something that I once referred to as "a turning point in human history." I still believe that, but I fear that human history may not be ready for it yet.

The Project is actually a combination of a number of different components. Many years ago, Albert Einstein and Nathan Rosen first developed the theory of the Einstein-Rosen Bridge, which some are now beginning to refer to as a wormhole, and the term by which I know it is familiar to you. Years later, they revisited the concept, fine-tuned and adjusted it as the basis for The Project. Albert also brought in a number of other ideas adapted to its development.

For example, it was initially theorized that a wormhole would not actually be traversable, due to its instability. Albert theorized, though, that a sustained sound wave of a certain frequency might interact with the fields in the wormhole, causing it to remain open. The sound wave must be absolutely pure and constant, to act as a torsion tensor, thus keeping the wormhole pure and constant as well. Maintaining that pure and constant wave, however, required an enormous, almost prohibitive amount of energy.

But Linus Pauling and Leo Szilard collaborated on a miniature nuclear reactor which could generate the power necessary to, not only create the wormhole, but to keep it open and traversable.

Others contributed to The Project in smaller ways, including Kurt Gödel, Edgar Lowenbaum and myself.

The prototype I built was small and, while the wormhole it created was not physically traversable, all images of past and future were able to be transmitted to me visually, in full and living detail. Having seen bits and pieces of your accomplishments, Oren, I must say that I've never been prouder of a family member, especially given the opposition that you must face, primarily, I know, from your father. As you do so, perhaps you may be encouraged by the words of my friend, Albert Einstein: "Highly developed spirits often encounter resistance from mediocre minds."

And now, as I have sadly but, I think, unavoidably dismantled the prototype, I hope the documentation, findings and schematics included herein will be helpful to you, should you choose to delve into these studies yourself.

Best of luck and much love to you, son. May you accomplish great things and find great happiness!

Your grandfather,
Wendell Oren Curtis

Our son was born at 8:47 on that sunny Sunday morning in January, the day I was supposed to die. Dr. Collins had saved the last towel from the stack that O.B.Wan had brought to wrap the baby in.

"Well done," Dr. Collins said to Becky as he smiled and handed the little bundle to her. "Just over four hours."

Becky was exhausted, but she smiled as she took the tiny creature in her arms. We both crowded together to be able to look at him. We counted fingers and toes – ten of each. We examined his features to see who he resembled – jury's still out on that.

But we couldn't stop smiling. Watching his tiny, delicate fingers grasping our big, chunky ones. Listening to the little noises he uttered. Delighting in the different faces he made. We had both fallen in love and were on a path that was sure to annoy the hell out of our friends.

As still, apparently, sometimes happened, a scripture from my past came to mind, from the book of Isaiah. "Then had thy peace been as a river, and thy righteousness as the waves of the sea." I glanced at Becky, then back down at the baby. I was definitely feeling a river of peace.

After spending some time with Becky, Dr. Collins determined that she was fine and would not need to make a trip to the hospital. It was about 10:00 when he left.

Becky and I were sitting together on the sofa, the baby in my arms, as O.B.Wan came into the living room.

"Well," he sighed as he dropped heavily into the easy chair that he had sat in the first day I met him and Sprach. "That's all done," he said.

"I'm sorry," Becky replied. "That must have been hard, turning your father in. Or even just facing him like that."

"It was, and it wasn't. We've been at each other's throats for years. We've never been close. But it's good to have it over." He looked at me. "Thank you, by the way."

"I didn't do anything," I said, surprised.

"You stood by me. It was an expression of solidarity, even though I know you had more important things on your mind, and I know you didn't know what you were getting yourself into."

"Well, it seemed like *you* knew."

He grinned.

"Once I tracked down and eliminated all of Sprach's sabotage," he related, "I was finally able to actually use STP. I started opening viewports – low-power wormholes," he said as an explanation to Becky, "view only, no interaction – using the coordinates that I had gotten from the road south of your house. I knew now that Sprach had always set it for 5:00 in the morning, so that's when I started it. And almost immediately, I saw it. And I realized that it was going to happen this morning.

"It was late, and I didn't want to wake you, so I decided that the thing to do would be to call you before it happened, delay you enough to keep you out of harm's way. After I decided on that, I," he paused and grinned again, "well, I couldn't quit. I suppose it sounds kind of narcissistic, but I was curious about what it was like to watch myself, like you had done on those mornings. So, while it was still running, I moved the coordinates over to here. I watched myself go about various routines down in the lab, and I got bored right away. I mean it was just me doing shit I do every day, so it lost its appeal pretty quickly.

"Then, I saw my father and Sprach arrive. I listened to his demands, saw myself resist him," he paused and took a breath, "and saw myself get shot in the head by thug number one. There were some things he said that added to suspicions I already had that he had killed his father.

"My grandfather's death had always been suspicious. The police had closed the case as an accident, but there were still some unanswered questions. A heavy bookcase had fallen on him and crushed him. It was enormous and sturdy. But there was no evidence that anybody else had been there, so they decided that he must have been holding on to one of the upper shelves, reaching for a book on a high shelf, and pulled it over.

"Well, both hoping and dreading that I was right, I called the Sheriff's Department and told them that I could give them a murderer if they would come over this morning. They were reluctant, questioned me quite a bit over the phone, and they finally agreed to send some deputies over and fit me out with a wire. They recorded the whole thing."

"So, you were supposed to die this morning, too."

"Apparently," he nodded. "No telling what kind of chaos is going to happen now, with *two* people who cheated destiny running around polluting the timeline."

I smiled grimly as I recalled my confrontation with Sprach about that.

"And to think," I said, "Sprach had actually been in the past, interacting with people, and potentially altering the timeline in a myriad different ways."

"Yeah," O.B.Wan said, shaking his head slowly. He seemed deep in thought. He looked up at me, and when he spoke, his voice was softer. "I just had the thought that I could open a viewport to the day my grandfather died, and actually see what happened.

"Can you imagine the impact this technology could have on criminal investigations? I wonder if it would be admissible in court."

"It would probably require a whole new set of legislation," Becky said.

"Actually," he said, "if I opened a traversable wormhole, I could even *prevent* crimes. Go back to the time when I knew a crime had been committed and prevent the person from committing it."

"Hmm," I said, "now I'm afraid it's starting to sound a little like a Philip K. Dick novel." Suddenly, a thought occurred to me.

"Hold on," I said, "you said you were going to call me and prevent me from heading into the accident. But you didn't call until I was right there."

"Yeah, I'm sorry about that. I told you I was up late doing all this. I never did get any sleep. By the time the deputies got me fitted out with the wire, I realized what time it was. I was afraid I was going to be too late.

"I rushed downstairs, calling your number as I ran. Fortunately, the equipment was still up and running in the lab. I was already setting the coordinates when you answered, and when you said you saw the gas truck, I knew I had to act fast. I engaged the opening of the bridge in the road in front of you, and the end of it in my backyard.

"I'm sorry to bring you here into the middle of all this mess with my father, but at the moment, it was all I could think of. And I knew the deputies were here, so I guess I thought it would be safer."

"Wow!" I said, realizing again how close we had come to death that morning.

"Thank you so much," Becky said earnestly. "We can never repay you for saving our lives."

"My pleasure," he said, a little shyly.

"You know," I said, "Becky used to make fun of my boring life and my daily routines." I looked at her next to me. Her smile was almost embarrassed, but she leaned against me affectionately. "After this morning, I'm kind of looking forward to resuming a more routine lifestyle."

"So, where did Dr. Collins come from?" Becky asked.

"He's an acquaintance of mine. And a neighbor. He just lives a couple of miles away. You might be surprised, but there's a growing number of doctors who make house calls, and he just happens to be one of them."

"Thank you for that, too," I said.

"Sure." He looked at the baby resting quietly in my arms. "So, what did you name him?"

"Well," Becky said, "Jack made a couple of less than stellar suggestions." I rolled my eyes at O.B.Wan.

"Calvin is not 'less than stellar'!"

O.B.Wan snorted.

"Calvin Hobbes?" he said. "I love it!" I cast a glance at Becky. "What was the other suggestion?" he asked.

"JackSimile," she said.

He nodded and smiled.

"A worthy candidate, but I can understand your rejection of it."

"She thought of William," I said, "her father's name."

"Naming him after his grandfather is a nice idea," he said, looking warmly at Becky. "William Hobbes."

"But in the end," I continued, "we decided on Oren."

He looked quickly at me, a look of surprise on his face. When he turned back to Becky, she was smiling and nodding.

"Guys," he said softly, "I don't know what to say."

"Ultimately," Becky said, "it's because of you that he's here. And us, for that matter. We'll never forget that."

"I'm honored. Thank you." He looked at little Oren again. "And his middle name?"

"Brandon," I replied. "Her father's middle name. I thought it was a little less common than William."

The almost sentimental look on his face slowly turned into a big smile.

"Another O.B."

Out the corner of my eye, I saw Becky look at me as the realization set in, but I avoided her gaze.

"Would you like to hold him?" I asked.

O.B.Wan looked at the baby, and smiled as he stood up.

"Come, my young Padawan."

www.ingramcontent.com/pod-product-compliance
Lightning Source LLC
Chambersburg PA
CBHW031338170626
46807CB00002B/760